"Giving up?"

Mockery edged Jake's voice, and Alix felt the by-now familiar sting of antagonism.

"Possibly." She was beginning to learn caution in dealing with Jake. She wasn't going to risk more insults than she had to.

"No more casual little questions? No more alluring swimsuits in the early morning?"

"No more insults from you. No more Captain Bligh orders. No more blisters and broken nails," she pointed out tartly.

Something sparkled in the blue of his eyes. "No story...."

Alix bit her lip. That was the problem. Was she ready to walk away from that? Was she going to let him scare her off just like that?

He seemed to follow her thoughts with uncanny ease. "Just how far *are* you willing to go to get this interview?"

Lynn Jacobs was born in Scotland, but has spent much of her life traveling. She went to school in the Far East and the United States and, although she now thinks she's settled in England, she can't guarantee it! Lynn has written stories for as long as she can remember. It was only a few years ago, however, that she first dared to submit one to a publisher. She enjoys sailing and riding, as well as lazing in the garden or on the beach with a good book.

RISK TO LOVE
Lynn Jacobs

Harlequin Books

TORONTO • NEW YORK • LONDON
AMSTERDAM • PARIS • SYDNEY • HAMBURG
STOCKHOLM • ATHENS • TOKYO • MILAN
MADRID • WARSAW • BUDAPEST • AUCKLAND

ISBN 0-373-17193-5

RISK TO LOVE

Copyright © 1993 by Lynn Jacobs.

CHAPTER ONE

HER eyes shielded by her sunglasses from the low glare of the early morning sun, Alix Bray lifted her gaze from the magazine article she had been browsing through and watched the man rowing ashore from the big yacht anchored in the bay. Now *there*, she thought, lips twitching in private amusement, is exactly what I imagine the writer of this rubbish means when she calls a man a 'hunk'. He had beached the small wooden dinghy and was dragging it ashore, its weight clearly no problem to him. She watched the muscles slide and tense under the deeply tanned skin of his back. He must be someone working on one of the boats out here. He certainly wasn't a local: few West Indians were well over six feet tall with blond hair bleached almost to whiteness by the sun. He half turned towards her and she found herself looking quickly away, conscious that she had been staring.

The trite words on the page in front of her made less sense than ever. She might be staring down at the page, but her eyes were seeing, like the afterglow of a lamp in a suddenly darkened room, the man at the water's edge. His face had strongly marked features and the jutting chin had a faintly piratical air. His torso had a light dusting of fair hair which arrowed down from the width of his chest across a lean stomach to where a pair of frayed and faded denim shorts rode low on his narrow hips. He wore nothing else, although when she looked up she saw that he had picked up a pair of scuffed leather sandals from the dinghy.

5

They were the only two people on the beach and he was going to pass not fifteen feet from her. Not even a sudden, absurd self-consciousness, like a child caught staring at an adult, was going to make her rude enough to pretend he didn't exist. After all, most of her colleagues were men, and any of them would be amazed to discover this hint of uncertainty in the assured Alix. She pushed her glasses up on to her dark auburn hair and squinted a little against the sun to smile with at least the appearance of confidence at the approaching stranger.

'Hello,' she said. 'Isn't it a wonderful morning?' Like every other morning in this tropical paradise, she supposed, but she had to say *something*.

He looked at her and grinned. It was an unexpectedly open and friendly smile and changed his rather dauntingly strong looks into something altogether more charming. And attractive. Her stomach felt oddly hollow as he changed direction and walked over to join her. He squatted easily beside her and she realised he was even bigger than she had first thought and wondered, wildly, if he really was some reincarnated buccaneer. Perhaps all those warnings about not talking to strangers still applied, even in places that called themselves tropical paradises.

His eyes surveyed her with a look which briefly made her wish the gauzy yellow shirt concealed her plain black swimsuit considerably more thoroughly. For a moment she thought he frowned, but then he looked away, to where she had been watching the many blues of the water as it deepened from turquoise to a blue so dark as to be nearly black. His gaze turned back to her and she realised as he spoke that he was American.

'It sure is lovely,' he agreed in a deep, quiet voice.

For a moment she couldn't think what he meant. Then she remembered her own comment. He was watching her now and she hoped, but wasn't at all sure, that it was the scenery he was talking about. His eyes were light blue, like the water where it became just too deep to stand comfortably. Was she already out of her depth? She pulled her glasses back down, shielding herself from whatever he might read in her eyes. Protectively, hoping he would see it only as a casual gesture, she sat up, hugging her knees. Some reflex made her need to defend herself from that expressionless but oddly penetrating gaze. She felt her body tighten uncomfortably and tossed the long, dark plait of her hair back over her shoulder in defiance.

This was ridiculous. It was a perfectly respectable, in fact positively modest costume, certainly nowhere near as revealing as some of the daringly cut styles she had seen on her first visit to the beach yesterday. What *was* there about this man?

He wasn't even looking at her any more. His eyes had dropped to the magazine lying discarded on the sand beside her and then he looked up, a touch of dismissive scorn in his gaze.

'You're enjoying that?' He nodded at the glossy cover and the strident headlines offering to improve everything from her figure to her sex life. There was even a token article on endangered species to show how environmentally aware the magazine was. From her rather sketchy acquaintance with its contents, Alix had already decided that the only endangered species it was really concerned with was the eligible male—and that was only in terms of how to capture him.

She shook her head to his question, even while she couldn't ignore the fact that an outstanding specimen of the species was lounging beside her. Not that she was interested. Her career was more important than some muscle-bound beach boy. 'No,' she told him. 'It's just something I picked up at the airport.'

'Typical cheap journalism,' he said scornfully.

No one expected men to admire that sort of women's magazine, and this one was certainly below the standard of most. It was only a casually dismissive comment, so what on earth was there in his voice to make her tense?

Whatever fleeting emotion had been there didn't last. He's going, Alix thought with a sudden sense of loss, but he was still looking down at her. 'You're staying over there?' he guessed, nodding to where the palm trees hid the hotel chalets.

'Yes. I just came down to the beach to enjoy it before it gets crowded.' She gestured at the emptiness, then, embarrassed by her own words, which must have sounded as though she wanted to get rid of him, added, 'I'm sorry. I suppose that sounds dreadfully selfish.'

He picked up the magazine she had left lying on the sand and handed it to her, a slow smile lurking in his eyes.

'Not really. I didn't come ashore at this hour because I was in any hurry to get to the shops. I wanted a walk and I like empty beaches too.'

She'd already begun to make a fool of herself. This blond stranger was too unsettling; it was time to go in. Besides, that last comment was probably a hint, even if hers hadn't been.

She smiled, her expression deliberately bright and non-committal. 'I'll leave you to it, then. It's probably getting on for breakfast-time at the hotel.'

Either he wasn't used to reading people's faces or he was seeing uncomfortably below the surface, because he didn't take any notice of her attempt at polite withdrawal.

'Why don't you walk with me? It's too fine a morning to go in yet and I'll only have to think about work if you desert me now.' The carefree grin contradicted the plaintive words. Alix couldn't help responding to it, and it *was* a lovely morning. Of course she should say no.

She had plenty to do today and he was probably used to picking up any lonely female tourists he happened to come across. She glanced at him again and found herself thinking that he probably didn't get many rejections. An unexpected and rare impulse to do something entirely frivolous seized her. Besides, when did she ever get the chance to give into temptation except on an unexpected jaunt like this? Surely she wasn't really taking much of a risk?

Hesitantly she looked up at him, again aware of his height, although she was not short. That endearing grin crossed his face, softening his expression, and she felt herself responding helplessly to its charm, even while telling herself she was behaving like an idiot.

'Come on,' he coaxed. 'Your things will be safe enough in my dinghy and you don't really think there's any rush for breakfast at half-past seven in the morning, do you?'

Alix couldn't help it. She had to smile back at him, admitting, 'I doubt if the dining-room staff are even fully awake yet.'

He took the towel and magazine from her, turning to his small boat. 'You're here with a boyfriend? Husband?' he suggested.

She glanced down at her ringless hands and wondered whether her answer mattered to him. No husband. No boyfriend. No one, really, since David's defection before their wedding, and that had been six years ago. 'No, I'm here on my own,' she answered honestly. He looked both surprised and curious, but she was glad when he didn't ask any more questions. She had no intention of saying anything about her private life, and this morning she didn't feel like talking about her work, or the challenging interview she would face this afternoon before her return tomorrow to the chilly dampness of London in March. 'What about you?' she wondered as he came back towards her. 'Is that your boat out there? Are there many of you on board?'

For a moment he hesitated and then he shook his head. 'I'm the only one on board. I prefer to travel and sail alone,' he told her.

'No encumbrances and a girl in every port?' she hazarded, only half teasing. He certainly wouldn't have any trouble finding the girls. And why should that worry her?

He chuckled. 'If I'd known you were in Guadeloupe, I'd have offered you the job here,' he told her.

Improbably, she found herself thinking that she just might have been tempted to accept. Aloud, she said, 'If I'd known pirates came marauding here at dawn, you wouldn't have had the chance.' It was unexpectedly heady fun to find herself indulging in the sort of light flirtation she thought she'd forgotten years ago. If she'd ever known about it.

The grin became distinctly devilish. 'Too late now: you've been captured.'

One large hand reached out and snared hers. The clasp was friendly and unthreatening, but she sensed its latent strength even as she felt the involuntary quickening of her pulse. Somehow she was unable to prevent herself returning the pressure of his fingers, but did manage to remind him lightly enough, 'Just a walk?'

She liked his quiet laugh. 'Just that. I'm not feeling strong enough for rape and pillage at the moment, or for dragging you off by your hair to my galleon. Although,' he added with an appreciative gleam in his eyes, 'you've certainly got the hair for it.'

The long plait of glossy brown hair hung almost to her waist. 'Yes, well, I'm not feeling weak enough to act the willing victim,' she told him judiciously, wondering just how far she was lying to them both. 'I'd kick and struggle and probably get sand all over your boat.'

If he ever did decide to carry anyone off, she rather doubted if kicking or struggling would do much good. 'Besides, I rather value my hair attached to my scalp,' she added.

'I can certainly see why,' he told her, and again she felt that disconcerting sense of self-consciousness. Surely she was years past blushing at the expression in a man's eyes or the tone of his voice? Or of thinking that they meant anything.

They walked together in silence for a while until they neared the end of the beach. Alix looked down at the white sand under her toes and ahead of her to where a rickety flight of wooden steps led upwards into the trees.

'Have you been up there?' he asked.

'No. I only arrived yesterday morning and I haven't had a chance to explore. Where does it go?'

He smiled, as though enjoying her enthusiasm. 'I'll show you. Hang on while I put on my sandals, then we'll go on up and out to the point together,' he suggested.

When he straightened it seemed only natural to take the hand he held out to her again. The warmth of his clasp was somehow both familiar and disturbing. Alix glanced over her shoulder. All that disturbed the smooth sweep of sand behind them were their own footprints.

'You wouldn't think there's a hotel full of tourists less than half a mile away, would you?' The deep voice echoed her thoughts, startling her. She hoped he hadn't been following them too closely; the idea of being alone on a tropical island with this man was something she was having trouble not lingering over. She turned back towards the steps.

'Give it another couple of hours and the beach umbrellas will be out in force,' she reminded him drily. Somehow it seemed important to break the curious spell of the moment.

His chuckle accepted her change of mood rather disconcertingly. 'Let's not waste time, then. Up you go.'

The first part of the climb was steep, but Alix was fit and did not find it difficult, though she suspected that, on his own, the man walking beside her might have taken it at a far faster pace. He was certainly untroubled by the rocky terrain and the growing heat of the morning.

They emerged at last on to the open, scrubby grass of the cliff's edge. To their left the little sheltered bay, the yacht anchored near its far side, glimmered peacefully in the sunlight, its waters pale blue and turquoise, darkened occasionally by small patches of weed on the white coral sand. But this was not the view which held Alix's attention, and her companion was already gazing the other way—out to the open sea.

She spoke her thoughts aloud. 'It's beautiful, but it's quite frightening, too.'

He turned to her, the hand which had clasped hers going round her waist in a gesture that was obviously intended to be reassuring rather than intimate, although her reaction to it was more complicated. But perhaps he hadn't felt that brief shiver which she hadn't been able to control. His voice, when he spoke, seemed thoughtful.

'Frightening? Yes. In the wrong mood the sea's stronger than anything human, and anyone who forgets that is a fool. But there are so many other moods, and so much magic, that no one could possibly discover them all.'

She heard the lift of eagerness. 'But you're going to have a damn good try?' she suggested.

The arm tightened on her waist as he chuckled lazily. 'I just might,' he admitted. He followed her gaze as she took in the view: an infinity of ocean, touched by odd currents and the wind's breath into patterns like watered silk, and the distant smudges that were other islands. 'Have you been to the West Indies before?' he wondered.

'Never,' she admitted. 'And I've not had a chance to see much in the short while I've been here. I was a bit tired when I arrived and I've been relaxing and soaking up atmosphere ever since.' She felt defensive, as though she ought to have made more effort in the short time since her arrival, but he didn't seem to condemn her laziness.

'Most people try to fit in all the sights at once and forget about the atmosphere,' he told her. 'And since you still look as though a light breeze would lift you off this cliff, I hate to think what a state you were in when you got off the plane.'

She had been pale, exhausted and tense. Keeping her place in a man's world might be exhilarating, but the past few years had taken more out of her than she wanted to admit. A good night's sleep and a lazy day had done a lot to help, but she was conscious that, beside his tanned fitness, she probably still looked frail. But she wasn't going to be blown anywhere now. Not while she was anchored to something as solid as this man's frame. He had drawn her slightly closer as he spoke and, because it seemed the most natural thing in the world, she found herself returning the loose embrace with her own arm around his waist. At first the warm touch of his muscled flesh beneath her palm made her tense. There was something very intimate about being held against him like this, but—unlike most of the men she had come across—he seemed content, not inclined to take advantage of the moment. Gradually she relaxed, although she could not quite still her awareness of the powerful body against her own.

'That's Antigua, over there.' He pointed with his free arm to the nearest island. 'Just a short day's sail away, but totally different from here. It's very British, and English Harbour is full of beautifully preserved buildings from Nelson's time.'

'While here is very French, very civilised and more concerned with good food and good living than with antiquities,' she reflected.

'That's right. That's what I love about these islands; they're so close to one another but so different, because each has its own history and traditions.'

He made it sound so fascinating. Alix wanted to hear more about his travels around the islands, but time was passing too fast. She sighed. The sun was fully up now. She could feel its heat through the thin fabric of her shirt. Reluctantly, she straightened. His arm, after a pause which might have existed only in her imagination, dropped from her waist.

'I really do have to go back to the hotel,' she said quietly, as though answering a question that he had not asked.

She looked up at him. The blue eyes held all the mystery and allure of the sea, but they were in a gentle mood. 'I know you do. How much longer are you here for?'

Instinctively she stiffened. Despite her thoughts of a few seconds ago her own wariness was too deep-seated to respond easily to whatever he might be suggesting. This morning had been fun; it would make a pleasant memory when she was back at her desk. And that was all.

'Another day or two,' she told him, being deliberately vague, hoping she sounded neither rude nor encouraging.

He raised his eyebrows. 'A bit short for a Caribbean holiday?'

Alix shrugged. She didn't feel like explaining just what she was doing here. She had watched too many people change their opinion of her when she told them about her job. For a moment she knew a sudden flare of impatience with its demands. She didn't want to spend today going over notes and preparing questions. But that was why she was here, she remembered with resignation. 'What about you?' she wondered aloud, the polite return of his question almost automatic.

'I've got some business to deal with.' His voice was hard and a sudden chill turned the pale eyes Arctic. Alix didn't envy whoever it was who had persuaded him to do something he found so distasteful to contemplate—and she was surprised that anyone had managed it. She shivered despite the sun, and he focused on her again, his smile apologising for the moment of impatience.

'Come on, I guess we'd better get back to the beach.'

He didn't move for a moment, however, and Alix found herself suddenly breathless, her heart beating hard in a way that had nothing at all to do with the steep climb they had shared. She couldn't look away. Was he going to kiss her? Did she want him to? He lifted one hand, tucking a long, escaping strand of hair back behind her ear. It was an oddly protective gesture and his hand lingered for a moment against the angle of her jaw. She could feel the softness of its palm as well as the faint calluses that boat-handling must have given him. She met the question in his eyes with her own wide and unsure. Crazily, she was tempted to turn her head slightly so that she could touch her lips to the base of the thumb which was almost absently tracing the line of her cheekbones. The absurd impulse made her look down in confusion and, half a second later, he took his hand away.

They walked back down the hill and along the beach almost in silence. Alix couldn't think of anything to say which would not come out as absurdly sentimental or revealing. It must be the effect of this place that had her thinking she had forged some sort of bond with this stranger. The sooner she got back to work, the sooner she would regain her normal self-control. It wasn't even worth exchanging names, because that would imply a future which didn't exist. She would fly home tomorrow and he, presumably, would cruise away to some other tropical island. The thought brought an unexpectedly sharp pang of regret.

They were back at the dinghy. He handed her the magazine and the towel and then stooped again, plucking something from the sand at the water's edge.

'Here,' he said. 'A souvenir.' The delicate convolutions of the perfect shell he placed on her palm seemed far too fragile ever to have coped with the power of the sea, and its soft colours glowed pink and ivory in the warm light. Alix stood there, helplessly holding it, not quite knowing what to say. His smile was lop-sided.

'Thanks for the walk,' he said at last. 'Go carefully.'

'Yes,' she agreed. 'And you.' It was hard to turn away, and she found her eyes held and trapped in the blue of his. He took a half-step towards her and fire flickered somewhere in the cool depths of his gaze. Then he stopped.

'Some of my pirate instincts are becoming assertive,' he told her drily. 'I just might fling you over my shoulder and carry you off to my boat after all if you don't make a run for it. Now.'

He was teasing, but there was a note of warning in the rich timbre of his voice that she hadn't heard before, and she wasn't entirely sure how to take it. For a second she wanted to challenge it, and damn the consequences, but just then she heard her name called.

'Alix!'

She turned and saw the elderly couple she had had dinner with the previous night standing by the trees in the distance, waving at her. Reluctantly she turned back to the man standing by the dinghy, and shrugged. 'I think I've just been rescued,' she said, not even attempting to hide her disappointment.

He too had seen the figures among the palms. Now he was watching Alix and, once again, something seemed to have changed in his face. The piratical image was, if anything, more marked than ever.

'I wouldn't be too sure of that,' he said quietly as he pushed the dinghy easily into the sea. '*Au revoir*,' he called, bending to the oars and sending the little boat quickly through the water.

She waved, but he was too intent on his task to wave back, and, uncertainly, she turned away to walk slowly back towards the hotel.

She lingered for only a few minutes' polite chat with the couple who had waved before leaving them to their morning stroll and returning to the small, palm-thatched cabin that was her room. Despite its deliberate external appearance of simplicity, the room inside was more luxurious than most accommodation she had found herself in when on assignment. As she stripped off her shirt and costume and stepped naked into the shower she found herself wondering what *his* accommodation was like on the boat. The yacht had seemed quite large from the shore, but then she knew nothing at all about sailing, and his casual references to trips between islands had sounded both glamorous and frightening. How on earth did he manage without a crew? And why? she added, frowning. Some risks just didn't appeal to her.

Even if the man himself did? Her dark eyes met the challenge of her own reflection, blurred by steam, as she stepped out of the shower and wrapped herself in a large white towel. Oh, yes. She wasn't an impressionable adolescent any more, but nor was she the embittered jilted fiancée who had spent years fighting to regain her self-respect while denying that any man would ever influence her again. So what was she? A successful twenty-seven-year-old journalist who just happened to choose to live alone. And who had reacted to a total stranger in a way she had forgotten was possible? Oh, shut up, Alix told the mocking image in the mirror, and turned her back

on it as she bundled the long, wet strands of her hair
into another towel. There were risks other than sailing
which she had no intention of courting.

She dressed quickly in white shorts and a bright pink
T-shirt. Breakfast was what she needed to settle an over-
active imagination. A couple of large cups of coffee
would put the encounter into perspective; she could tuck
it away, like the shell which now lay on the small table
beside her bed, with her other memories and think about
it later on as part of the unexpected charm of the West
Indies. Nothing, after all, had happened. She really
would be the archetypal spinster if she couldn't admit
that a man was good-looking. It didn't have to mean
that she wanted to do anything about it. Besides, she
had work to do.

By midday she had almost forgotten her uncharacteristic behaviour on the beach. What was demanding her
attention, and increasing her irritation, was the time it
had taken to place a call to the London office of her
newspaper and the fact that the only phone she had been
offered was just off the hotel's reception area, with very
limited privacy.

'Bill?'

'Yes.' The familiar curtness of her boss's voice greeted
her. 'Have you got that interview yet?'

Typical. No enquiry about her health or whether she
was enjoying herself. Not that she'd expected anything
else from Bill. In his office, at least, he was all professionalism—and Alix was usually glad of it.

'No.' Her reply was as direct as his question. 'We're
meeting this afternoon. Have you managed to get the
information I wanted or do I just go ahead with the
"Jake Hunter: Man of Mystery" line?' Her evident revulsion from the cliché prompted a bark of laughter from
her editor.

'Sorry, love. That's all I've got. Something might come in later on today—I'll fax it to the hotel if it does.' At least the hotel had that facility, whatever the other defects of its telephone system. She might still discover something to pad out the insubstantial knowledge she held.

'So I've got to interview an entrepreneur who takes over unlikely businesses and turns them into even more improbable money-spinners, who's managed to turn around a failing *Japanese-owned* consortium and double its profits in a year and could come from the Boston aristocracy or the slums of Chicago but no one seems to know which, with just a flimsy bundle of notes, speculation and insubstantial gossip to back me up?' she demanded.

Jake Hunter's progress through the American business world in the past six years had been meteoric, but his dazzling flamboyance in the market had shed no light at all on his background. She hadn't even been able to find a good photograph. The only one she'd come across was a grainy and poorly focused group shot, and the caption had been singularly unhelpful about which of the five men was Jake Hunter. Privately, Alix had a bet with herself in favour of the plump, balding man in the centre. He had appeared to be in his mid-forties and Hunter was surely unlikely to be younger than that, which ruled out two of the other figures; nor was he likely to be either of the other two, elderly men—one of whom she knew by sight anyway.

Bill's brusque tones cut across her memories. 'That's it,' he agreed in the tone with which he habitually demanded the impossible. He might be Uncle Bill in private, and her godfather, but he'd never done her any favours in the office, nor had she wanted them. It was enough that he'd given her a job when she would have taken anything, not excluding floor-scrubbing. If she was now the paper's business editor, no one, not even in the maliciously competitive world of journalism, believed that her post had come from anything but her own determination and talent. Not that that stopped her feeling as though Bill was expecting her to part the Red Sea without divine assistance.

'All I've got,' she reminded him, 'is a letter from someone in his publicity department offering me the possibility of an interview—whatever that means—and a heap of Press clippings that tell me what everyone else knows: that he's a man who makes things happen.'

'And makes money,' her boss added unnecessarily. 'Look, Alix, if he's moving into the British market we want to know it, and you've got nearer to him than anyone else so far.'

'Getting near someone that elusive is *not* going to be easy,' she said drily. 'He'll probably disappear as soon as he knows who I am.'

'He promised that interview,' Bill reminded her.

'His publicity assistant did,' she reminded him. 'I haven't heard a word from the man himself. I just wish I had a bit more information to go on,' she added, frowning.

'You've got all that anyone else seems to know. Don't worry, I'm sure you'll charm him.'

'Oh, yes. You know I just love being charming,' she snapped with more than a hint of irritation. She hadn't specialised in financial journalism by accident; it suited her to be away from the areas of the Press where her looks might mislead people—*men*—into thinking that glamour, gossip and intrigue held any appeal at all. And few people knew better than Bill exactly why she mistrusted all that those words implied. After all, he had watched her struggle to rebuild her life without David.

A long-distance chuckle acknowledged what she had left unsaid. 'Don't worry, girl; I've got faith in you.'

From Bill that was a tribute which almost left her speechless. Her voice softened. 'Thanks. I'll discover all—even if I have to *ooze* charm,' she teased.

'Any way that works, girl.' The moment's sympathy was gone, and so was Bill—he seldom bothered with polite, time-wasting farewells. The message had been delivered and there was no point in saying anything else. Not that Alix took that last comment seriously. Her paper's reputation for accurate information had nothing at all to do with the more dubious tactics of some of the more popular and speculative journals.

Slowly she replaced the receiver and turned away. It had really been a wasted call and she might as well go back to her notes.

As she walked quickly across the reception area someone disappeared through a doorway to her right. Alix turned at once and then stopped, mocking herself. If she was going to let every tall, fair man she glimpsed remind her of this morning's encounter, then it really was time she pulled herself together and got her mind back on her job. A very private smile touched her mouth.

In a chair not far away a young man who had been watching her speculatively wondered for a moment if that glimpse of laughter on the delicately high-cheek-boned face was an invitation. Without it she had seemed somehow remote, despite her stunning looks, but that impish tilt to her full mouth lent intriguing life to her face. Reluctantly, he decided that the expression wasn't intended for him. Besides, his girlfriend and the rest of their party were waiting for him in the bar. With a long backward glance at Alix he collected his things and left.

Quite unaware of the other man's existence, Alix walked back to her cabin, letting her thoughts linger for a moment on the incredulous response of Bill if he could have seen her this morning: allowing herself to be picked up by a stranger whose name she never discovered and letting his image drive out thoughts of urgent work afterwards did not fit anything he knew of her. Reluctantly she dismissed the image of the bronzed pirate with eyes the colour of the sea, and forced her attention back to the notes she was meant to be studying.

Jake Hunter's publicity director had told her that she could meet his employer in the hotel in which she was now staying. When she had first arrived she had scanned the guests with interest, wondering if Hunter was among them. It hadn't taken her long to decide that they were all genuine tourists. He might not even be staying on the island, she realised, or else he might have a house of his own here. The lack of precise knowledge was infuriating. It was so much easier to interview someone when you had at least *some* idea of the personality you were likely to encounter.

Acknowledging at last that she knew as much as anyone on the subject, and that anyway it was too late to worry, she closed her notebook and began to change for the meeting.

It didn't take long. She seldom fussed about her appearance—after all, for most of her adult life it had been more of a handicap than an asset to her. She had decided when she packed to come here that the linen suit would be appropriately businesslike. The amber silk blouse was an old favourite which went with several other outfits. Confining her hair into a coil at the nape of her neck, she grimaced without much pleasure at her reflection in the mirror. She'd do. As she turned away and picked up the high-heeled shoes she had not worn since arriving on the island, she was unconscious of the way the short straight skirt emphasised the length of her legs and flattered her slim figure while the colour of the blouse set off her clear complexion. Without doing more than glance at the mirror to confirm that she looked neat and professional and that her light make-up was unsmudged by the heat of the afternoon, Alix picked up her notebook and recorder and left the room. The knot of excitement, which had once been fear, with which she always met a challenge tightened in her stomach. A glance at her watch told her she had five minutes to get to the main hotel and her appointment with Jake Hunter. Perfect.

CHAPTER TWO

HEELS clicking smartly on the cool tiled floor, Alix walked over to the room indicated by the receptionist and knocked.

'Come in!' called a male voice with a peremptory edge and something else in it that briefly shook her assurance, making her hesitate before she grasped the knob and turned it.

She took two steps into the room and stopped. Behind her the door swung softly closed. In front of her, wearing a light jacket over an open-necked sports shirt and looking as piratical as ever, was the stranger from the beach.

'You!' she exclaimed, knowing and not caring that her voice and face betrayed the sudden surge of pleasure which she couldn't control. 'What are you doing here? I was expecting——'

'Jake Hunter,' he finished, cutting ruthlessly across her words, and she realised that he had not moved to greet her, nor had he responded to her smile. 'Very nicely done, Ms Bray,' he added with unmistakable scorn.

'But I don't understand,' Alix protested. It was as though the world had shifted suddenly into some unfamiliar and hostile pattern. Her friendly companion of this morning was watching her from across the desk, leaning back in his chair as he surveyed her coldly. She didn't want her growing conviction confirmed. 'Do you mean *you're*——?'

Again he did not let her finish. 'Of course I am. Now can we cut the act?' Heavy sarcasm edged his voice.

Act? Which of them was acting? Alix remembered with unwelcome clarity that he hadn't been in the least surprised when she entered the small room. 'Do you mean you knew who I was all along?' she demanded.

He shook his head impatiently. 'No. Your disguise was very convincing, Ms Bray.' The look in his cold eyes remembered the bathing costume and flimsy shirt and dismissed them as some siren's tawdry outfit. Alix began to feel a saving swell of anger. Just who did this man think he was?

'But you weren't surprised to see me just now,' she reminded him.

'Correct. I'm quite capable of doing a little research of my own. I heard the old guy call you Alix and that made me wonder, especially when I remembered how short you'd said your visit would be. I decided it would do no harm to check it out. If you weren't Alix Bray, then it still might be useful to know your name.'

Useful. Her blood chilled at the thought of the 'use' he might have expected after their walk together. She was a fool. Hadn't she had her lesson about men already?

He must have seen something in the stiff whiteness of her face. 'Don't pretend you didn't know who I was when you arranged that oh, so touching encounter on the beach,' he snapped.

He clearly wasn't going to offer her a chair, so Alix walked across to the desk and took the seat facing him, hoping that only her determination showed and not the doubt about whether her legs would hold her.

'I hadn't the faintest idea who you were, Mr Hunter,' she said as coolly as rage and self-disgust at her naïveté would let her. 'If I had, I would have introduced myself.'

His dismissive shrug expressed contempt and disbelief. Without straightening, he steepled his fingers in front of him, staring at her across them as though at some predictable but unpleasant phenomenon. His eyes,

Alix realised, were almost glass-clear in the room's harsh light. Whatever laughter or sympathy she had thought she had read in them in the morning sunlight was gone without trace. When he spoke again it was as though she had said nothing.

'A typical woman's trick. I suppose you wrote that garbage you were wallowing in when I turned up?' he added with scorn.

'Of course I didn't.' He had touched a scar that she hadn't known was still raw and, infuriatingly, she heard her voice crack slightly. Teeth gritted, she spoke again, with deliberate control. 'If you're so good at research I'd have thought you'd have read my work before agreeing to this interview.' The years had taught her that submission fuelled scorn; defiance was her only weapon. But this was not a battle she had expected to be fighting here. Not with *him*.

He hesitated fractionally, but there was no doubt in his voice when he spoke. 'Oh, I did. I looked at Alix Bray's work all right, but there's nothing in your column to indicate that Alix Bray is female. If she is. There isn't even a photograph with *your* by-line.'

The sarcastic stress on the pronoun cast doubt on her very identity and turned her into an opportunist gossip-seeker. It didn't help that the accusation held a tiny shred of truth. She and Bill had originally made a conscious decision not to print a picture; too many people would have used it, rather than her writing, as something to judge her by. Now, although she still valued the occasional privacy the absence of a picture supplied, she seldom thought about it. Everyone in the trade knew who—and what—Alix Bray was.

'Your research was a little inadequate,' she commented, more coolly than she felt. 'It's no secret that the business editor of the Recorder is a woman.'

'That still doesn't justify your act this morning.' His voice was coldly dismissive.

'It wasn't an act,' she repeated. Six years fighting to hold her own in a tough profession had taught her to keep her temper, but this time she wasn't sure how much longer she could hang on to its shreds. 'I'm not the only one who doesn't make photographs freely available, Mr Hunter,' she reminded him. The brittle, even quality of her voice masked the urge to fling her recorder down on the floor, or at him, and walk out. Instead, she put it carefully on the desk between them.

He sat up, the front legs of his chair hitting the floor with a decisive thud; and pointed at the machine. 'You won't need *that*,' he told her.

As simple as that? She was a woman and therefore not worth talking to. She had met the attitude before, but it was never any easier to cope with. And the contrast between this blond autocrat and the devil-may-care companion of this morning was beginning to make her feel slightly ill. This man was shattering his own image into worthless fragments. He was destroying a memory that had been precious and now he was trying to destroy her. Let him. She had little to lose. Failure might anger Bill, but it wouldn't cost her her job. She left the recorder where it was.

'Tell me, Mr Hunter, if you despise journalists so much, why on earth did you agree to see me?' Sweetness barely concealed the acid in her voice. 'It's not really your style, after all.'

His own anger seemed to be back under control, but the cynicism was unabated. 'I had my reasons.'

'And now that you've discovered who I am, everything's cancelled?' concluded Alix.

'That's right.' His voice lacked any inflexion at all, even when he added, 'And you've had a nice little West Indian holiday at your paper's expense, so you haven't

anything to complain about, have you? After all——'
and suddenly the ice was knife-sharp '—it's hardly your
fault if you didn't manage to get quite as "near" to me
as you planned, is it? You certainly "oozed enough
charm" this morning to convince the most cynical man
of your sincerity.' Abruptly he stood up. 'Next time,
though, I'd advise you to make your phone calls to your
gossip-hungry friends just a little more private.'

He strode out of the room before Alix could begin to
think how to defend herself from his misunderstanding
of that phone call to Bill. So she hadn't been seeing romantic fantasies when she thought she'd glimpsed him!

Romantic fantasies? If that was what Jake Hunter had
been to her a few hours ago, he had certainly managed
to change his image now. Of all the arrogant, pigheaded, narrow-minded... The list of adjectives ran out
long before Alix's temper cooled. Whatever he'd over-
heard, he'd obviously been determined to put the worst
possible construction on her behaviour this morning, and
the idea of simply asking for an explanation had clearly
never even entered his good-looking and utterly conceited skull. Well, he could ask all he liked now; she
wouldn't tell him anything if he *begged*.

Not that it seemed as though she was likely to have
the chance. There was no sign of him at all as she left
the private room, although she'd half expected to see a
trail of damage left in his wake. Like a hurricane. His
departure had, after all, had some of the elemental fury
of a force of nature.

Her own rage cooled slowly and she didn't much care
for what she saw when she was able to think rationally
again. She had blown it. For six years she had prided
herself on her professionalism, and now she'd wrecked
the most important interview she'd had in years because
of a couple of hours' self-indulgence this morning. She
should have known it would be a mistake. It was never

really work which hit you in the face or cut you down just when you thought life was under control. It had happened before and she had vowed then never to let her personal life get out of control. This morning she had acted like an adolescent fool and, as a result, had been dismissed like one.

The knock on her door roused her briefly from bitter self-recrimination.

'Yes?' she wondered wearily. She didn't even begin to hope it might be Jake Hunter offering her another chance. People like that didn't give second chances. Besides, her temper hadn't cooled *that* much; she still wished he'd stayed round long enough for her to throw something at him.

It wasn't Jake. A young West Indian she remembered vaguely was holding out an envelope.

'This arrived for you just now, Miss Bray. By the fax machine,' he told her, proud of his hotel's erratic technology.

Inside the envelope was a single sheet of paper from Bill. Too little, too late, she thought wryly, thanking the lad who went off, evidently pleased with her generous tip.

She held the flimsy paper for a long moment before looking at it. It hardly seemed worth it since she had already lost her chance.

In the end it was impossible to ignore Bill's notes. Journalists were at least as entitled as women to curiosity, weren't they? She wasn't sure whether it was as a journalist or as a woman that she read and re-read the brief facts before her. Bill still hadn't discovered much about Jake Hunter's roots—'Definitely not Boston blue blood' was the only information that emerged there— but what held Alix's attention, raising more questions than it answered, was the fact that Jake had once been married to Ellen Carter. It might be a name that was

only slightly known in England, but Alix had spent
enough time in New York and watched enough American
television to have a vivid image of the tall, blonde woman
with the reputation for daring clothes and gossip-hungry
interviews whose chat show had occupied a prime-time
slot on one of the major channels for the past four years.

'Married two years. Divorced five.' So Ellen Carter
had risen to fame after the marriage had broken up?
Alix wondered if that was why it had failed, why Jake
had been so hostile this afternoon; did he disapprove of
working women on principle? It was an attitude she had
come across often enough, but it didn't seem to fit the
little she knew of him. She was sure she'd read somewhere that there were a number of female executives in
his firms, and, besides, there had seemed something
almost vindictively personal in the strength of his anger,
not just the unpleasantly familiar patronising of the
chauvinist. Not that she wanted to draw any parallels
between herself and Ms Carter. She had watched the
woman's show a couple of times and found herself faintly
repelled by its mixture of gossip and innuendo.

So she had a detail about Jake Hunter's private life.
Where did that get her? Nowhere. The only consolation
was that the knowledge of his marriage and divorce could
have had no influence on what had happened that
afternoon. Perhaps it was time to phone Bill and tell
him that she'd failed.

No. It was a long time since she'd allowed herself to
be intimidated by a man's insinuations that she owed her
job to her looks. And if Jake Hunter had any of the
acuteness he was generally credited with, surely he'd realise what nonsense it was as soon as he'd calmed down.
She still couldn't work out exactly what there had been
about that morning's confusion of identity to produce
such an irrational reaction—unless he was vain enough
to *expect* people to recognise him, despite his carefully

guarded privacy?—but she did know that if she backed down now he might really start to believe his own accusations. She'd give him a couple of hours and then go out looking for him. Surely there weren't that many places on a small island where someone with his distinctive looks could disappear?

The decision enabled Alix to do most of her packing in a more positive frame of mind. That brief and near-disastrous confusion of private and professional lives was over. At least she now knew what to expect when she insisted on that interview she'd been offered. No more idiotic and emotional responses. It didn't matter what he thought of her; she was only doing her job, after all. Nor was there any point in calling Bill until she had something positive to report. Soon.

The problem with good resolutions and positive planning, Alix thought several hours later as she gazed blankly out towards the darkness of the sea from the restaurant terrace, was that some things tended to get left out of the calculations. Like the yacht that had been anchored out there this morning and which was there no longer.

In her determination to track down Jake Hunter she had asked several of the hotel's employees about his whereabouts. Most had shrugged, explaining that he wasn't a guest and they knew nothing of him, but one had gone outside and pointed out to the bay. 'His boat's gone,' he had told her, and it was only then that she remembered that he had had the easiest of escapes from the island.

Alix turned away from the view and the memory of the bitter taste of defeat, a far from ladylike expression crossing her mind. She didn't like losing. Especially not to conceited egotists with a macho self-image and too much money.

There seemed to be nothing left to do but finish packing ready to catch the plane tomorrow. The queue for the telephone was worse than ever; Bill could wait until he saw her before hearing what a mess she'd made of things. Bad news could always wait. Angry with herself, but still unable to work out what she could have done to stop Jake Hunter walking out on the interview, Alix went to bed and slept badly.

She was up early next morning with no inclination at all for a walk along the deserted beach—beside the equally deserted sea. It took only a few minutes to finish packing and ask the receptionist to call for a taxi. The hotel had lost almost all its charm somewhere round the middle of yesterday afternoon, and Alix decided she would infinitely prefer the mindless chatter and petty discomfort of the airport to another hour of this deceptive luxury.

It was as she was carrying her bags to the cab that the boy—the same one, she noted with wry amusement, whom she had tipped so lavishly for bringing her the fax yesterday—caught her attention.

'Miss Bray?' he asked, lifting her single suitcase into the back of the waiting taxi.

'Yes?' She was only half listening, still wondering what else she could have done to salvage something from that disastrous 'interview' with Jake.

'I hear you've been looking for Mr Hunter?'

Alix's attention, along with all her professional instincts, sharpened suddenly. 'Yes?' she repeated in an altogether different voice.

'He's on his boat,' the boy told her confidently.

Her own surge of hope died. 'I know that,' she said, trying not to sound too sour. 'And the boat's probably halfway to Florida by now.'

'No, miss. It's at the marina. I saw her there this morning.' The lad's expression was triumphant. And why not? decided Alix, reaching for her purse and unable to prevent her own answering smile.

'Thanks. Tell the driver to take me there first, will you?'

'Sure thing, Miss Bray. Mr Hunter's a nice man. Enjoy yourself.'

The grin that accompanied these parting words left Alix's cheeks flaming. She was tempted to call the lad back and explain exactly why she wanted to see Jake Hunter and, further, that he was anything but a 'nice' man. The taxi driver's impatience and her own common sense stopped her. She had a feeling that no explanation of hers would do anything except widen the grin on the boy's face.

When the taxi drew up at the small harbour, Alix dismissed it and then looked around in bewilderment. There seemed to be yachts everywhere. How on earth was she going to identify his wretched boat when she didn't even know its name?

Fortunately, an enquiry of a man working on a rather battered-looking fishing-boat was immediately helpful. 'Jake's boat? Sure. That's the big ketch down the end of the jetty there.'

She had no idea at all what a ketch was but 'down the end of the jetty' was a sleek-looking white yacht with two masts and decks of scrubbed wood. The name *Shearwater* was picked out in blue along the back of the yacht and a narrow blue line running along the top plank of the hull accentuated the gleam of white paint and varnish.

Big? It certainly seemed larger than most of the other yachts in the harbour, but Alix's idea of safety at sea ran more along the lines of the *Queen Elizabeth II*. She preferred not to think of the *Titanic*; they were in the Caribbean, after all. No icebergs here.

She picked her way carefully along the rather rickety wooden planking of the jetty, regretting the impulse—had it been vanity or a need to rebuild the professional veneer which had taken such a blow yesterday?—that had led her to dress up for the flight home. Specifically, she regretted the elegant Italian sandals whose heels seemed to catch in every flaw in the planking and whose straps were pinching both her heels and her toes.

At last she was hesitating on the dock beside the boat which had been pointed out to her, uncertain whether she should just step on board. How did you knock on something that had no obvious door? Tentatively, feeling like an idiot, she rapped on the deck. Surely he would hear that if he was in there? For some minutes nothing happened and she had a fleeting hope that there would be no response and she could be on the plane back to civilisation in a couple of hours. Then a hatch slid back and Jake stepped on deck.

Alix's mouth went dry and, despite herself, she wanted to smile at him. He was dressed exactly as he had been the previous morning and that memory briefly over-shadowed their subsequent, shattering encounter. Beads of water clung to his chest and arms and his hair was combed flat, darkened to bronze by its wetness. He must have just come from a shower, she realised, her pulse quickening involuntarily at the thought of him casually tugging on the brief shorts over his naked hips when he heard her knock. Then his blue eyes met hers and she revised all her previous thoughts about icebergs. Clearly, *he* had not forgotten yesterday afternoon.

'What are *you* doing here?' he demanded curtly. 'I said all I wanted to yesterday.'

'I didn't,' Alix couldn't stop herself replying. Some trace of her feelings must have shown through her dry tones, because Jake's eyebrows flickered as though sur-prised at her defiance.

'So?' He was offering no encouragement.

'So you still haven't given me that interview,' she reminded him. 'Since you didn't stick around at the hotel, I decided I'd see you on your yacht.'

For a moment he seemed to hesitate, and Alix thought she might have won. Relief and elation warred in her, then Jake's expression hardened. 'Too bad,' he said abruptly. 'I'm going sailing.'

There were moments, Alix realised, when sheer exasperation could make you do things you would never contemplate in a more rational state. This was one of them.

'Then I'll come with you,' she heard herself saying in a voice of steely calm.

That eyebrow lifted infuriatingly again, but he did not move from his lazy pose on the deck.

'Not in those shoes, you won't,' he drawled, eyeing the offending sandals and their sharp high heels.

For one moment longer Alix held that insulting blue gaze which was daring her to lose her temper and walk off, then she bent down and deliberately undid the narrow straps of the shoes and straightened, holding them dangling at arm's length. Meeting the challenge of his gaze again, she simply let them go, not even blinking at the satisfying splash they made as they hit the water.

Something that might have been reluctant amusement tugged at his mobile mouth, but Alix wasn't interested in entertaining the wretched man; she just wanted to get on with her job.

'*Now* can I come on board?' she asked in saccharine tones.

He looked her over for a long moment and, despite her rising annoyance and determination, she found it hard not to colour.

'What would you do if I objected to the skirt as well?' he wondered in a mild voice that did not deceive her for a moment.

Well, she had started this fight and she wasn't ready to back down yet. Not quite.

'Do you?' She hoped her nervousness about his answer didn't show. Bravado had its limits, and she had no intention of indulging in a strip-tease for his benefit.

The pause went on entirely too long for Alix's composure and made her acutely aware of how far the short, straight skirt revealed her long legs.

'I've nothing against it as a skirt,' he began at last, and she started to relax—until he added, 'But it's not exactly what I'd call sailing gear.' That was it. She had done everything she intended to, and that didn't include losing any more of her clothes. She bent to pick up her suitcase and walk away with whatever dignity her bare feet would allow her.

'Coward.' The soft drawl of the single word stopped her in her tracks. She turned. He was still leaning against the wire rigging and this time there was no mistaking the derision-laced amusement in his face. 'Running away?' he taunted.

'It's called a strategic withdrawal,' she managed with a fair assumption of calm.

'Sure looks like retreat to me,' he decided.

Temper took over. After all, there was nothing left to lose. 'I don't care what it looks like. I'm leaving. I'm a journalist and if I can't have the interview I came for— and was offered,' she reminded him, 'I've got plenty of other work waiting.'

'None this interesting,' he interrupted with infuriating truth, adding, 'For a journalist you don't have much staying power.'

'I have plenty,' she snapped. 'I just find walking on water a bit difficult, and you're "going sailing".' She invested the phrase with as much contempt as she could, reducing it to a childish game.

The sneer didn't seem to affect him much. 'I thought you wanted to come with me,' he pointed out.

'I want—or rather my *editor* wants—to interview you. It's my job.' Unspoken but quite explicit was the conviction that nothing else on earth would make her want to exchange another word with him.

'I do deals. It's *my* job.' He hadn't moved from his relaxed position by the rigging, but there was a new alertness in his voice that made Alix cautious.

'What do you mean?'

'Negotiations. If you can convince me that it's worth my while, I'll give you that interview.'

'And just how do I do that?' Suspicion which she did not even attempt to hide edged her voice.

A smile whose charm she did not trust at all tugged at one corner of his mouth. 'Just what you wanted; come sailing with me,' he offered.

She should have been triumphant; wasn't he offering exactly what she wanted? Instead she felt as though the ground was shifting beneath her feet—and the planking of the marina jetty wasn't to blame. Why did she feel as though control of this situation had suddenly changed hands?

'So I get an interview. What do you expect to get out of this?' she demanded, wishing somehow that she was safely back in a taxi and heading for the airport with only Bill's anger to worry about.

'Entertainment?' he suggested blandly, and his cool gaze surveyed her with no attempt at all to hide the insult in his eyes.

So he expected her to run true to type—as he saw it— and be willing to offer anything, including herself, to get what she wanted. A gauntlet had been thrown down. Against all her better judgement, Alix knew she was

going to pick it up. And so, to judge by the glint in his
eyes, did Jake. Even as a child she had got into trouble
for never refusing a dare. She looked up at him, and
around at the unfamiliar surroundings of ropes and sails
and confusing rigging where he seemed so utterly at
home, and knew what she ought to do. If she had any
sense left at all she'd give him a flat 'No!' and take the
next taxi to the airport. She tilted her chin to confront
him, read his expectation of her continued retreat in his
smile, and rebelled.

'You've got a deal,' she said, far more calmly than
she felt.

Wordlessly, he reached out a hand for her case, taking
it from her as though it weighed nothing.

'I should have known you'd do anything for a story,'
he commented drily. 'You can take the skirt off down
below. Come on,' he added, impatience clear in his voice
as she hesitated, all her doubts resurfacing, redoubled.
Why did she have the feeling that she had been manipu-
lated into exactly this situation? She wasn't quite sure
what he'd meant by that last remark, but if it was the
way it had sounded she was going to have to put him
straight. Now.

'Mr Hunter?'

He turned, irritation tightening his mouth. 'Now
what? If you've changed your mind you can stay ashore,
but you've got less than five minutes before you'll need
to swim for it.'

Alix glared back at him. 'I haven't changed my mind.
I just want to make sure you know that all I want from
you is an interview.'

An eyebrow quirked mockingly. 'And I said we'd
negotiate. Now, have you made up your mind or shall
I put this back on the dock?' He gestured towards
her case.

She felt the heat flaring in her cheeks. She should have known she couldn't win an exchange like that with someone like him. She only hoped that at least the message had been received and understood. 'I don't change my mind very easily, Mr Hunter,' she said through gritted teeth.

'You can call me Jake,' he said casually, and then ruined what she might have interpreted as an offer of a truce by adding, 'as long as *you* remember that I don't change my opinions about people.' It was obviously another warning. She thought about pointing out that he had managed to change his mind about her fast enough yesterday, but decided to wait until he wasn't in a position to order her off the boat. Surely even *he* wouldn't throw her overboard, no matter how much he despised her? Stifling her doubts, she stepped carefully through the narrow opening in the guard rails and on to the deck.

It was a relief when the boat only dipped slightly; she had been half afraid of a sudden lurch which would topple her ignominiously at his feet. He was watching her with a guarded expression, as though something about her puzzled him. In the end he said nothing, but took her bag and walked over to the hatch. Lacking any other instructions, Alix followed, her lips tightening. Clearly Jake Hunter was not going to go out of his way to make this outing a pleasant one. What on earth had she let herself in for? she thought wildly. Surely even professional dedication had its limits?

Down a short, ladder-like flight of steps they emerged into a spacious room where Alix was both surprised and pleased to discover that she could stand upright. Even Jake's hair barely brushed the wooden ceiling, although, in his current mood, his presence was enough to make any room seem cramped.

'This is the saloon—the living area,' he told her. 'The galley—kitchen to you—is there.' He indicated a neat little area with a stove and a stainless steel sink with plates above it in specially designed shelves. 'Can you cook?'

'I enjoy it,' she told him honestly. And at least that might be something familiar in this bewildering environment with its confusing language.

He looked sceptical but said, 'We'll see,' as he led her through the saloon and opened the door to a small cabin. 'You can change in here,' he told her. 'There's a shower and toilet opposite.' He indicated another door and went into the cabin with her case.

She followed him in automatically. It wasn't until he had dumped the bag unceremoniously on the narrow bunk and turned to leave that she realised just how small the tiny room was. Without thinking, she reached out to prevent a collision and found her palms flat against the wall of his chest.

She should have snatched them away, but she could feel his heart beating fast beneath the golden warmth of his tanned skin. She looked up. Sweat beaded his upper lip and for a moment something flickered in the light eyes. Then his own hands came up, taking her wrists and holding her away.

'Excuse me,' he said calmly, letting her go and brushing past her into the main cabin. Alix stood there for a long moment, rubbing her wrists as though that cool grip had bruised them. Then, impatiently, she turned to her bag, yanking the zip open and rummaging for something more practical than a suit.

There was no sign of Jake in the saloon when she had finished, so she went back on deck. He was at the front of the boat, doing something with a confusing-looking heap of sails and rope. He glanced up as she approached.

'What do you want me to do?' she asked, and cursed herself for giving him the opening.

His lips twitched in what might have been the beginning of a mocking smile, but the expected offensive suggestion didn't emerge. 'Just stay out of my way,' he said curtly. 'You can begin to learn what's happening here when we're under way,' he added before turning back to his task. The strong fingers were moving with deft expertise, linking the sail to a wire stay, checking each link with casual assurance.

When everything was done to his apparent satisfaction he reached down to a switch in the cockpit and the engine roared into life. Alix was both surprised and relieved to hear it; somehow it made conditions seem a little less primitive. He glanced up at her, a derisive glint in his eyes making her wonder if he had read her thoughts, but he only pointed to a bench seat and said, 'You'd better sit there,' before bending to free the mooring ropes.

The yacht moved away from the jetty without apparent fuss. Alix could feel as well as hear the slap of the waves against the boat's side. Perhaps this wouldn't be so bad after all. Then Jake called her over.

'Here. Take this.' He indicated the wheel he had been handling with practised ease.

'Me?' She wasn't at all sure she was ready for this. Then she saw the impatience darkening his eyes and reached out for the sun-warmed varnish of the wooden spokes. Her tentative gesture and suddenly tight clasp on the wheel seemed to amuse him.

'It's not going to bite you,' he assured her. 'Just keep her pointing towards the harbour entrance.' He gestured to the gap between the cliffs. Since there were no other boats near and the gap seemed quite wide, Alix relaxed slightly. He watched for a moment and then nodded as though reluctantly satisfied. 'I'll get the sails ready,' he said and walked away before she could protest.

The next few minutes were a confused blur. Alix kept
her grip tight on the wheel and her eyes fixed firmly on
the harbour entrance while Jake busied himself with the
tangle of ropes. Occasionally he'd shout an order at her
and she'd alter the direction of the boat at his bidding
with no idea at all of what she was meant to be achieving.
All round her masses of sail started to lift in billowing
heaps while ropes slammed and clattered increasingly
noisily. And sailing was meant to be a *peaceful* hobby?
Then Jake was beside her in the cockpit again.

'I'll take her now.' Relieved, Alix gladly surrendered
the wheel. He turned it slightly, reached out with a free
hand to pull a rope more tightly round a winch, and
then switched off the engine.

The boat tilted slightly, then steadied, all noise but the
rush of water suddenly ceasing. Braced for disaster, Alix
cautiously relaxed and looked around her with dawning
surprise and delight. The sails were full and steady and
what had seemed like utter chaos had suddenly become
a strangely beautiful symmetry which was clearly op-
erating in harmony with all the natural forces around
them. Where the engine had helped the yacht batter its
way across the waves, the sails seemed to be lifting it,
allowing it to cut cleanly through the water.

'It's lovely!' she exclaimed involuntarily. Jake glanced
sideways at her as though surprised.

'You'll be out of the way on the foredeck,' he told her
bluntly, gesturing to the front of the boat.

It seemed prudent, for the moment at least, to ignore
the tone and accept the order. She had already achieved
far more than she had expected—after all, there was
surely no way the great Jake Hunter could avoid talking
to her now? She preferred not to contemplate exactly
what the situation was going to cost her—except for a
missed flight. She was willing to put up with his resentment if she got the story she had come for, she told

herself firmly as she began to realise just how isolated they were—and how helpless she was in an environment about which she knew nothing. At least she hadn't yet disgraced herself by being sick. She could just imagine his sarcastic comments when she started to turn green. The very thought made her determined that if it was possible to prevent seasickness by sheer will-power she was going to do just that.

She was just beginning to wonder whether she had been wrong and Jake *was* going to ignore her entirely when she heard a voice from the back of the boat demanding, 'Have you gone to sleep up there?'

Startled, she looked back towards him. At the wheel he looked more like a pirate than ever. 'No,' she called back, reluctant to move.

'Then come back here for a moment. This isn't a pleasure cruise, you know.'

She sighed. For a short while she had almost fooled herself that it was. Reality was altogether less appealing. She moved carefully back along the deck, realising as she did so that her body was already adjusting automatically to the yacht's motion.

When she rejoined him she stepped awkwardly into the cockpit behind him. She didn't want any more accidental collisions with all the disturbing currents that the last one had generated. He looked over his shoulder as she passed him, one quizzically flaring eyebrow seeming to note, and mock, her caution.

'You said you could cook?' he said abruptly.

'I can.' The doubt in his voice made her own answer defiant.

He shrugged. 'Well, I don't suppose you can go far wrong with what's on board. Do you think you can organise lunch?'

She hadn't realised how much time had passed. A glimpse at the clock down below confirmed that she had spent far longer than she had thought just watching the sea go past. Grudgingly, she had to admit that Jake had done all the work so far and that it was only fair that she should prepare the meal—whatever the tone of voice in which he asked for it.

As she looked through the cupboards she realised what that last remark had meant. Lunch would have to be sandwiches or nothing; there was little other food available.

He took the tray from her as she negotiated the steps back to the deck. 'Thanks,' she muttered. Then looked around, alarmed. 'Who's sailing the boat?'

Something that might have been real amusement lightened his face as he put the tray down in a niche where it wouldn't break free. 'George,' he said. Her bewilderment must have shown, because he indicated some elaborate equipment at the rear of the boat. 'The self-steering gear,' he explained.

So that was how he was able to sail long distances alone. He had a sort of mechanical crew. Cautiously she began to relax, looking around her with growing interest. 'Why's she called *Shearwater*?' she asked eventually when he didn't seem in any hurry to banish her to the foredeck again or relieve George at the wheel.

'It's a particularly graceful type of sea-bird,' he answered easily enough. 'It seemed appropriate.'

'It's perfect,' Alix agreed. Somehow she would never think of the yacht as an anonymous 'thing' again after today. 'How long have you had her?'

'Five years,' he admitted. The quick frown at her question made her ready to defend herself, but his comment held mockery rather than irritation. 'Why the inquisition? Have you got that recorder concealed about you somewhere?'

Since she was wearing shorts and a T-shirt over her bathing costume, no answer was necessary. The look he had given her as he spoke left her in no doubt that he knew exactly how little she could conceal. With an effort, she stifled the urge to go below and pull on a pair of jeans at least—anything, in fact, as a barrier to the appraisal in the clear eyes which, she saw, had taken on the darker blue of the sea around them. He's only trying to intimidate you, she reminded herself, uncomfortably aware how easily he had succeeded. But he didn't have to realise that.

'No,' she said coolly, 'but it won't take me a moment to fetch it.'

'Don't bother.' His voice was curt. 'I'm still not convinced you're going to get that interview.'

'Then why did you agree to it in the first place?' Impatience and curiosity made her ask the question that had puzzled her since his first violent reaction to her identity. Even before then she'd been surprised when someone so notoriously inaccessible had agreed to see her.

'I didn't.'

'But I've got a letter——'

'From my publicity director,' Jake interrupted ruthlessly. 'He seemed to think that it would be a good idea to get a little advance publicity if I'm to operate in Britain. He didn't check with me first.'

So someone had thought he could take Jake's reactions for granted. Alix winced. She had seen the glint in his eyes and didn't envy the unfortunate man who was doubtless now out of a job—even if he'd survived the verbal flaying Jake had inflicted first.

'You sacked him?' she assumed.

His eyebrows quirked. 'No.' Her surprise must have shown. 'No—I didn't like the way he handled it, but the idea made some sort of sense, rightly applied. I just made it clear where responsibility for my privacy lay and told him to try his ideas in some other area of PR. He'll do well,' Jake added judiciously.

So the flaying had gone ahead, but not the dismissal? Somehow that only made Alix more uneasy. That sort of control even, perhaps especially, when he was angry made Jake Hunter every bit as dangerous as she had feared—and made her equally determined not to back down.

'But you decided to cancel the interview anyway when you found out I was a woman?' she challenged.

'When I found out what sort of woman you are.' The statement was flat, rejecting any argument, but she had had enough of the prima donna act.

She had lost her flight back to England, thrown away a perfectly good—if uncomfortable—pair of shoes, and was stuck on a small boat in the middle of the ocean with an uncooperative tycoon who seemed to feel he could be as rude as he liked. 'So just who *would* you give one to?' she demanded incautiously. 'Your ex-wife?'

CHAPTER THREE

ALIX knew it was a mistake as soon as she had spoken.

Jake's eyes froze and she backed involuntarily away from the cold fury she saw in them, feeling the hard, varnished edge of the cockpit pressing into her back.

'And just what the *hell* do you know about my wife?' The very quietness of his voice made him more dangerous than if he had shouted at her.

'Very little,' she admitted, hoping that he didn't hear the slight tremor in her words. Somehow she had touched a very raw nerve. 'But I have watched Ellen Carter's TV show and I do know that you and she were once married.'

'Then you also know that's no longer the case. And I certainly don't have anything to say to you, or anyone else in the Press, about it or anything else in my private life.' The slammed door couldn't have been more obvious. He didn't have to add, 'Do I make myself clear?'

'Perfectly. I'll even agree to stop nagging you for an interview. For the moment.' Anything, she discovered, to take that cold mask from his face, that look which made her feel oddly aware not only of his power and anger but also, with an instinctive certainty she could neither explain nor question, of a wholly unexpected vulnerability.

He didn't move, but she sensed the relaxation of brutally tightened muscles, and some of the ice left his eyes. His voice was dry. 'I'm relieved to hear it. In that case——' he leaned back and picked up the glass of fresh lime juice she had brought out with the sandwiches '—have you any other questions?'

47

One had occurred to her rather forcibly as the island they had left shrank to a shadow on the horizon behind them. 'I did wonder where we were going,' she admitted.

A chuckle she had not heard since yesterday morning's walk surprised her. 'I'd thought about Bermuda,' he told her, adding in a different tone, 'It'll give us plenty of time to "negotiate".'

Bermuda! That was thousands of miles away! Just what sort of maniacal kidnap attempt had she got herself into? Then she caught the glint in his eyes at the same time as she remembered the state of his store cupboards. 'You're good at fishing?' she suggested, hoping without much conviction that he had missed her first reaction.

'Not that good,' he admitted with a wry grin. 'Look.' He pointed to something ahead of the boat. Alix had to lean across him to see where he was pointing. She felt the warmth of the sun on his bare skin and for a moment her senses could focus on nothing clearly except his nearness. 'Over there.' There was a hint of impatience in his voice now. The landmass ahead of the yacht was quite clear, although still too far off for any details to be visible. 'That's Antigua,' he explained as she retreated to the safety of her original seat and looked questioningly at him. Uncomfortably she remembered standing on a clifftop, his arm about her waist, as he indicated the same island to her. Perhaps he was remembering the same thing, because his expression was suddenly shuttered, his voice curt. 'We should be there in another two or three hours. *If* we stop lazing around. Perhaps it's time you learned something about sailing.'

The evident scepticism in his voice was all the challenge she needed. 'Good idea,' she said firmly, trying to suppress the suspicion that he was planning to get even with her for forcing herself on the boat.

An hour later the suspicion was a certainty. She had known sailing wasn't just a matter of lying around on deck, but did he *have* to make it such hard work? He seemed to be making her prepare for every possible eventuality even though they both knew they'd be in port soon.

'Damn,' she muttered, not for the first time, as another nail broke on the sail hank she was fastening.

'Aren't you ready yet?' The impatient voice from the cockpit made her grit her teeth. She'd see him in hell before she'd admit she had a problem, but surely he could lend just one of his much stronger hands to help her with these wretched fastenings? With a feeling of triumph, she managed to fit the last one. Now all she had to do was hoist the thing. It flapped and clattered as she hauled on the rope and then, inevitably, jammed. Muttering something she was glad no one else could hear, she gave a vicious yank. Incredibly, the sail soared smoothly upwards, filling with wind and lifting *Shearwater*'s bow, transforming her previous rather gentle progress to a swift motion which justified her name.

Looking up at the billowing mass of white sail, Alix realised, I did that. Suddenly sailing was beginning to make sense. The feeling of satisfaction wasn't even diminished by the sardonic amusement on Jake's face when she rejoined him.

'Now you've finally managed that, you can take the wheel again,' he told her.

No congratulations, no thanks, just one more challenge to try to master and the growing conviction that he was just waiting for her to give up. Did she want to? Until today she'd never set foot on anything smaller than a cross-Channel ferry and soon she'd be back in a way of life that had nothing at all to do with ocean sailing, so wasn't she being an idiot to let him goad her into action? Then she reminded herself of the interview that Bill was waiting impatiently to print. If there was still the slightest chance of persuading Jake into letting her have it, she'd willingly sacrifice every remaining fingernail.

By the time they anchored in Antigua she was feeling a sense of achievement that had nothing at all to do with her job and which she was certainly not going to admit to Jake. For a novice, she decided, she hadn't done too badly at all, and English Harbour itself was certainly worth the trip, with its succession of wide, sheltered bays and the cluster of restored eighteenth-century dock buildings. She could hardly wait to explore.

It was early evening before everything on the boat was tidied to Jake's satisfaction. She watched as he stared thoughtfully towards the shore, then he turned and asked mildly enough, 'What does your vast culinary skill suggest the ship's larder will run to for dinner?' His voice held little optimism.

Alix didn't even need to think about it. She knew the contents of his cupboards. 'Eggs. Boiled, scrambled or poached. If you're lucky I might be able to find you a slice of bread for toast.'

He regarded her thoughtfully as though he'd expected nothing better. If he was going to blame her for his own lack of supplies she had no intention of letting him get away with it, and she braced herself for his comment. Whether or not he read something in her face she couldn't tell. All he said was, 'Too many eggs are bad for you. Besides, I know how long those have been there. Looks like we're eating out. Ready in an hour?'

It might be phrased as a question, but Alix was rapidly learning to recognise an order when she heard one. Besides, she was ravenously hungry. A combination of nervous tension and a day in the open had left her hungrier than she'd been in years. She wasn't quite sure what she'd have done if he'd opted for scrambled eggs, and was glad she didn't have to find out.

Jake didn't say how dressed up she was expected to be for this meal, but she should at least change from her shorts. Frowning, she looked through her limited selection of clothes. Clearly her outfit couldn't include high heels, nor was she going to be fool enough to attempt to climb in and out of a dinghy in a skirt. In the end she found a pair of white jeans and a white camisole top over which she could wear the baggy yellow shirt she'd used as a cover-up. She tied a broad silk belt around her slender waist and brushed her hair loose from its plait before tying it back with a long yellow scarf.

The tiny mirror in the equally tiny bathroom was no help at all. She wasn't even sure if her hair was tidy and it was impossible to see both eyes at once to check that her make-up was even. Alix gave a short sigh of exasperation and picked up her lipstick, replacing it slowly as she realised just what she was doing. She had spent the last fifty minutes dressing for dinner with Jake as though preparing for an important date. She must be mad. The more care she took, the more he would assume he had been right about her. And, anyway, why on earth should she *want* to impress him? He had shown himself to be overbearing, prejudiced and arrogant—everything she most disliked in men. But he hadn't been like that at first, her memory insisted on pointing out. Isn't that the man you're dressing for? She didn't want to dress for *any* man. All she wanted was a decent meal and an early night. Defiantly, she brushed lipstick on her mouth and turned away from the mirror without a backward glance.

Jake was waiting on deck. He was wearing blue jeans faded almost to whiteness and a short-sleeved white cotton shirt. There was no reason for such ordinary clothes to make Alix nervous, except that she would have had to be blind not to acknowledge that nothing he wore could make him look ordinary. His mouth tightened briefly when he noticed the shirt she wore, and she wondered if he was reminded of their first encounter. Too bad, she decided defiantly, but found herself relaxing when he made no comment. He did surprise her, however, by offering a hand as she stepped down into the yacht's small dinghy.

They wandered for a while around the old harbour buildings in the rapidly fading light before going into a dockyard hotel. It was busy with yachtsmen from all over the world, many of whom greeted Jake with easy camaraderie and an unconscious respect which told Alix just how highly he was regarded as a yachtsman among this crowd of experts.

'How many of them know you as Jake Hunter the entrepreneur?' she couldn't help wondering aloud after a bowl of rich chowder had blunted the edge of her appetite. The question was a mistake. The familiar shuttered look, which had been missing from his expression all evening, told her to mind her own business.

'Some may. People tend not to interfere in each other's lives here.' Journalists were clearly not people. 'Anyway,' he went on, his eyes pale and derisive, 'surely you realised that it's my glamorous partner they're wondering about? And coveting. Aren't you flattered?'

'Flattered? If that's the sort of admiration that appeals to you, you'd better take up one of the offers that your friends' partners seem more than willing to make,' she snapped back. She hadn't missed the glances cast Jake's way by more than one of the women present.

'Perhaps I will,' he told her harshly, and Alix found that her appetite had suddenly gone. She didn't believe he meant what he said; he had spoken only to hurt. The problem was how easily he had succeeded. If only she knew who the real Jake Hunter was—the sensitive companion of the beach or the calculating and brutal man whom she had met later that day? The latter seemed to be dominant for most of the time, but, just when she thought him most intolerable, she would catch a glimpse of the other side. Was he truly dual-natured, or was some part of it an act? And, if so, which?

At the moment she would have liked nothing better than to walk out, but it didn't take the glint of anticipation in his face to remind her that she couldn't row the dinghy and had nowhere else to go. Cornered, she lifted her chin and regarded him with as much indifference as she could.

'If I were you, I'd pick the one in red in the corner over there,' she suggested. 'Her partner doesn't look much of a threat.' He followed her glance. The woman in question was clearly exasperated by a boyfriend who had obviously overindulged before coming out and was now finding it hard to concentrate on anything at all.

Unexpectedly, Jake chuckled. 'I'll pass, thanks. With those shoes she'll puncture the decks, and her nails look lethal.'

'You could get a nasty scratch,' Alix agreed solemnly, looking at the long talons painted to match the dress. She felt much better.

'You'd better sheathe your claws, too,' Jake warned, but the cold distance had gone from his voice and her own laughter mingled with his, even if, for one giddy moment, she had had a vision of her own nails, now filed short, against the heat of his bare skin.

The rest of the meal passed in relative harmony which lasted until they were back on board *Shearwater*. In the main cabin, Jake turned and offered her a night-cap. Alix shook her head.

'No, thanks, I'm beat.' She stretched and yawned. 'I'm sorry, all that sea air seems to have gone to my head.' It couldn't have been the wine at dinner—she'd only had a single glass.

Jake nodded. 'It gets you like that at first. You'd better turn in.'

Nodding agreement, she drifted sleepily towards her cabin door. Then she remembered something she had wondered about earlier. 'Where on earth do you sleep, Jake?' Hers was the only cabin she had seen so far.

'Alone.' The voice was ice, rejecting an offer she hadn't even made. 'My cabin is aft—at the back of the boat,' he clarified before she could say anything, 'and it's strictly off limits.'

'I'm delighted to hear it,' she managed to retort through sleep-fuddled shock, and was glad to be able to slam the door of her own cabin loudly behind her.

Of all the pigheaded, conceited men, she thought, wrenching the scarf from her hair and brushing out its wind-blown tangles with a vigour which brought tears to her eyes. He was impossible—a typical tycoon who thought his money could buy anything. He seemed willing to put the worst possible interpretation on everything she said or did, and she had to be mad to think for a moment that he was going to agree to any sort of interview. And that was *all* she wanted from him, she insisted; anything else was just an emotional response brought on by overwork and tension. *Any* attractive man would have had a similar effect on her. The derisive comment from her subconscious could just be ignored.

Fortunately that last flare-up between them didn't prevent her dropping into the most satisfying eight hours' sleep she'd had in months. She would happily have extended it, but the imperative rap on her door made that impossible.

'Coffee's made,' he called over her protest.

She emerged cautiously from her cabin, bundled in an over-sized T-shirt, her hair still tousled from sleep. She hadn't been able to read his mood from his call, but rather hoped he'd found urgent business on deck after summoning her. Unfortunately, he hadn't. He was fully dressed, looked depressingly alert, and was seated at the cabin table. He rose as she entered, taking in her appearance with a single comprehensive glance and offering her a mug to match the one he already held.

'Take this. You look as though you need it. I thought you were a morning person?'

Was that a reference to the walk on the beach? If it was, it was safest to ignore it. She didn't feel up to sparring with him. Yet. Taking the coffee with real gratitude, she muttered, with what dignity she could, 'I wake up slowly,' and sipped the mercifully strong brew.

He finished his own drink quickly and moved to the steps leading up to the deck. 'Call me when you're awake. *When* your brain's functioning again,' he added with heartless brutality, and left her alone.

A shower eventually completed what the coffee had started, and Alix swiftly plaited her hair, pulled on jeans and T-shirt, picked up her sunglasses, and joined Jake on deck. He was leaning against the rail, staring at the shore, a preoccupied, rather distant expression on his face which didn't change when he turned round and saw her. She wasn't quite sure what the look meant, but said, as brightly as she could manage, 'I think the coffee's taken effect at last.'

He didn't respond to her smile. So that was to be the way of it? Alix supposed she had been an idiot to think he might be in a more civilised mood this morning.

He straightened, frowning. 'What are your plans?' he demanded abruptly.

Somehow she hadn't got round to making any. Yesterday's impulsive decision to come with Jake had altered everything, but, she realised despondently, achieved very little. She shrugged. 'I suppose I can get a flight back to England from here as easily as from Guadeloupe,' she admitted.

'Giving up?' Mockery edged his voice and she felt the by now familiar sting of responsive antagonism.

'Possibly.' She was beginning to learn caution in dealing with Jake. Specifically, she didn't trust his moods and was certainly not going to risk more insults than she had to.

'No more casual little questions? No more alluringly demure swimsuits in the early morning?' he goaded.

'No more insults from you. No more Captain Bligh orders. No more blisters and broken nails,' she pointed out tartly.

Something sparked in the blue of his eyes.

'No story.'

Alix bit her lip. That was the problem. Was she ready to give up? How much risk was she really running in continuing their 'deal'? She sensed that he wasn't going to use his physical strength against her; it was a battle of wits he was offering, one which he expected to win. Was she going to let him run her off just like that?

He seemed to have followed her thoughts with uncanny ease. 'Just how far *are* you willing to go to get this interview?' he wondered, and the very doubt in his voice was provocation enough.

She returned his stare, glad that he couldn't read anything her eyes might reveal behind their dark glasses, and then looked around her.

'I've come this far,' she said slowly, wondering just how crazy she had become as her gesture took in the surroundings of English Harbour, so different from Guadeloupe. 'I'll risk going a little further. Unless,' she added, rather more sharply than she had intended, as she saw him straighten purposefully, 'it involves "oozing charm" over you.'

Surprisingly, Jake flung back his head and laughed aloud. Then he sobered. 'If you mean that, then how about coming sailing?'

Alix was immediately suspicious. 'I thought we'd done that yesterday.'

'Didn't you enjoy it?'

'Yes.' To her surprise, she *had* enjoyed it. Despite the blisters. 'But that's not the point——'

'Scared?' he suggested.

'No! Of course not!' Not of sailing, certainly, and she wasn't even going to consider anything else.

'Well, then . . . ?' he coaxed.

'I thought you preferred to sail alone,' she reminded him. 'Why go sailing with me?'

He ran his hand through his unruly fair hair and shrugged. 'Masochism, probably,' he said wryly. 'But I thought *you* wanted an interview. We'd only be away three or four days.'

Blast him; he was using that interview as bait, knowing quite well that she wasn't going to give up while he still held out a chance. But why he should apparently *want* her to take the bait, since he clearly hadn't changed his mind about her, made absolutely no sense at all. Or none that she wanted to analyse too closely. For all his flippancy, the look in his eyes was not without calculation; but she had come this far safely, hadn't she?

'All right, then,' she decided, feeling as though she was stepping into the lion's den. 'Let's go sailing.'

Sailing, however, had to wait until they'd stocked up the nearly empty food lockers, and Jake explained that this was best done in St John's, the island's capital. He led the way out of the dockyard gates towards the busy crowds around the buses and taxis parked in the wide open space there.

He looked down at Alix. 'I suppose we'd better take a taxi.'

She was disappointed. 'Can't we go in by bus?' She looked at the many locals jostling for places. 'Or don't they like the tourists using them?'

The look he gave her was enigmatic, but all he said was, 'We can take a bus.'

Standing in the aisle of the overcrowded bus beside Jake, Alix found herself constantly swaying against him until, as she stumbled and almost fell on a particularly sharp corner, she felt his arm go round her waist, holding her hard against him. Startled, she looked up; there was nothing but impatient exasperation in his face. She tried to pull away, but she might as well have been pushing at a steel barrier, except that steel did not have the warmth of his bare arm, felt through the cotton of her shirt, and no inanimate barrier would have been as uncomfortably disturbing as the weight of his hips, against which she was drawn.

'If you keep wriggling like that, you'll be in trouble.' The mocking voice was pitched for her ears only, but its warning held her still even more effectively than the arm around her waist. The heat that scorched her and quickened her pulse had nothing at all to do with the bright sunlight outside.

A large West Indian woman in the seat beside them said something incomprehensible in the local patois. Alix heard Jake's chuckle, but his grip didn't loosen, and she was glad she didn't understand either the woman's comment or Jake's reply, at which the woman had laughed aloud, nudging her neighbour and grinning up at Alix.

Eventually, after a ride which had begun to seem interminable, they arrived at their dusty quayside destination and everyone somehow managed to tumble out with their parcels. Jake took his arm from around Alix just as she was about to protest that she no longer needed any support. There was something very intimate about the caressing way he let it brush across her back as he released her, but a glance at the challenging tilt to his chin and the half-smile on his lips made her decide not to say anything. She joined the crowd outside and looked around. Out in the bay an elegant white cruiser liner was anchored; ashore, all was colour and bustle and confusion.

Jake touched her arm to draw her attention. 'We might as well split up. I'll get the bits I need for the boat and you get the food, OK?' He barely gave her time to nod. Splitting up was beginning to seem like an excellent idea. He was pointing down the street. 'The supermarket's on the main street, two blocks in that direction. The fish market's in that covered building on the quayside and you can see where the produce stalls are.' All around them were women selling heaped piles of glowing tomatoes, aubergines and grapefruit as well as bundles of green vegetables, corn and potatoes and small sacks of charcoal.

Alix looked at the chaotic scene. 'Do you want chicken or goat for dinner?' she asked drily. Legs tied together, chickens flapped helplessly by one stall; by another a couple of young goats bleated in a melancholy way.

Jake's tone matched hers. 'Whichever you prefer. Just don't get blood on the decks.' She wouldn't. Any meat was definitely coming from the supermarket and would probably be frozen. 'Will two hours be enough?' he asked. Clearly he was impatient to be off on his own business. 'I'll meet you back here,' he added and had turned away almost before she had finished nodding agreement.

She watched him walk off, greeting some of the men working on an upturned boat and receiving wide grins in reply. In other circumstances he would have made an ideal guide to the chaos of the town, Alix realised. As it was, though, it was a relief to be away from him for a while. *Shearwater* was surprisingly spacious, but it was too dominated by his presence, and the frequently flaring antagonism and awareness between them had made the

past twenty-four hours emotionally exhausting.
Purposefully, she walked briskly off in the opposite direction from the one he had taken.

In fact the town wasn't difficult to get round. It was
built on a basic grid pattern and most of the shops she
needed were clustered together. She took some time to
explore, but eventually realised that the heat was becoming sultry and the shopping was still to be done.
Starvation was unlikely to improve Jake's mood.

She left the supermarket cradling two enormous and
over-full brown paper sacks and somehow managed to
top them up with some fresh fruit as she passed the stalls.
Just as she was wondering whether there was any way
she could add some tomatoes to her haul, she realised
someone had come up behind her. Jake, she thought.
For once simple relief at the solution to her immediate
problem outweighed her usual, more complicated reaction to his presence.

A second later she realised it wasn't Jake at all. The
man attempting to relieve her of her bags might have
been as tall, but this overweight figure in slightly scuffed
naval whites, smelling strongly of sweat and beer, was
no one she had ever met in her life before, or wanted
to.

'Leave those alone,' she snapped, hanging on to the
precarious parcels.

'Aw, c'mon, love,' the drink-thickened voice insisted
as he swayed closer. 'Lemme carry them. Li'l lady like
you shouldn't be carrying 'em,' he confided, smiling at
her, showing uneven, stained teeth.

'No, I can manage.' But not against his obvious
strength if he lost his temper. The bags were going to
shred in a moment anyway under his fumbling clasp.
Alix looked quickly at the woman keeping the stall she
had left, but she must have found business elsewhere.
Perhaps it was unwise to interfere in the disputes of

tourists. 'Let me go!' She heard the shrill note in her own voice as she flinched from the hot touch of his hand on her wrist and wondered how long she could keep her growing panic under control. Wasn't there *someone* in all this crowd who could see that she was in trouble?

'Shouldn't be carrying them bags,' the pest repeated with evident determination. 'Let's you'n'me go for a drink. Nice cool beer,' he decided, and repeated the offer as though pleased with the inspiration.

He'd had more than enough already. She couldn't pull away, so she stood as still as she could and repeated, with what she hoped was the voice of cool dismissal, 'No, thanks. I can manage. Please let go.' Did that 'please' have too much desperation in it?

'I believe the lady asked you to let go.' The flat American drawl could belong to only one person. Unable to control a surge of relief, Alix watched Jake step towards the tipsy sailor.

'Who 'r' you?' the man slurred, reluctant to surrender his prize.

'The lady's with me.' Jake spoke again. There was no inflexion at all in his voice, but something in it made the drunk's eyes focus blearily on him. 'I told you to let her go,' Jake reminded him. Alix could only see his profile, but its iron determination was clear even to her, and something in his eyes made the other man flinch and step back a pace, releasing his grip. For a moment Alix remembered her image of Jake as pirate; just so he would crush the first sign of mutiny with the sheer force of his personality. She doubted if he often had to resort to the violence that he could probably deliver with devastating effect. She wondered if he had the same effect on an obstinate group of board members. Probably. For once she was glad of it.

The drunk took another step backwards, well out of the long reach of Jake's fists, then shrugged, muttering defiantly over his shoulder as he turned and shambled away. Alix heard him above the noise of the crowd. 'Should take more care of 'er. Shouldn' let her carry them bags. Ain't right.'

The persistent idea carried grumblingly across the market-place. Alix couldn't subdue a sudden giggle, more the product of nervous relief than any real amusement, then she looked up to meet her rescuer's cold glare.

'Can't you stay out of trouble?' he demanded unfairly. 'If you must encourage every man who passes by, don't you think you'd better learn how to cope when someone takes you up on the offer?' The sheer unfairness of the attack left Alix speechless. Humiliating tears stung her eyes. With her arms full of parcels she could only blink rapidly and hope her dark glasses hid her reaction. He was still staring down at her as though contemplating continuing what the sailor had started. Her silence seemed only to infuriate him. 'What would you have done if Mrs Thomas hadn't seen what was happening and found me?' he demanded.

The old lady from the fruit stall beamed as though unaware of the electricity that crackled between them. 'I seen you come off the bus this morning,' she confided. 'When that man grab you, I find Mr Jake. He sort him out good,' she explained, sounding slightly disappointed that Jake hadn't resorted to his fists.

'Thank you, Mrs Thomas. I'm very grateful,' Alix managed, her voice brittle with unshed tears. If she said any more Jake would really be able to gloat over her typical female weakness. Mrs Thomas, however, seemed to understand. She gave an even broader smile, added a large bag of tomatoes to Alix's battered paper sacks, and turned to Jake.

'You see you take her home now, Mr Jake,' she ordered severely.

'I will,' he agreed, although the dry severity of his voice didn't suggest that he was about to offer much sympathy. He glanced over at Alix. 'Come on. My stuff's over there.' He pointed to where a young boy cheerfully guarded a small heap of parcels.

'And you carry those bags for her, too,' Mrs Thomas instructed. Hurray for the sisterhood of women, Alix decided as Jake obediently took the groceries from her aching arms. A faint crease in his cheek and an ironic twist to his lips suggested the first softening of his mood.

'I was going to,' he said mildly. Beside him, Alix rubbed her wrist, grateful to be relieved of the burden. A single, unexpected oath escaped Jake. Alix looked up sharply. What had she done now? But Jake was watching the movement of her hand. 'Did that bastard hurt you?' he demanded.

She shook her head and managed a shaky laugh. 'No. The bags got a bit heavy, that's all.'

She thought he muttered something else, but she didn't quite catch it. 'Come on,' he said aloud. 'Let's get back to the boat.' Impatience was evident in his voice.

Alix managed a quick farewell and repeated thanks to Mrs Thomas and then had to move fast to follow in the wake left by Jake's progress through the crowd. When they reached the heap of his purchases he said curtly, 'Wait here,' and disappeared again before she could protest.

Minutes later a taxi drew up and Jake got out, holding the door for her. 'In,' was the laconic command.

'But what about the bus——?' she began. She had looked forward to the journey home.

'Blast the bus. We've far too much to carry and, besides, you're more likely to stay out of trouble like this. Get in.'

She got. She wanted to be angry and tell him what she really thought of his pigheaded arrogance, but somehow her legs weren't feeling quite as supportive as they ought to be and the relatively cool shade of the cab's interior was a welcome relief. She'd let him know her feelings when she felt stronger. Besides, she did owe him some thanks for the rescue, however he had handled it.

As the boot slammed down on the last of their shopping and he slid into the seat next to her, she turned and tried, 'Thanks for your help.'

When all it got was a shrug and, 'I think you're safer at sea,' she didn't even have the energy to think of a come-back, never mind voice it.

By the time they were back on the boat Alix was feeling completely wrung out. Jake turned to look at her as she sprawled on the cushioned seat of the cockpit. Warily she returned his gaze.

'You look hot,' he observed at last, idly brushing back a lock of hair that had fallen over his forehead.

It was one-thirty in the afternoon of a tropical day, she had just come from a close encounter with a drunken sailor, and she had carried what felt like half the contents of a supermarket across the town.

She returned his look with well-feigned surprise of her own. 'It must be the weather,' she decided in her most English tones, looking up at the cloudless blue of the sky.

His laughter was the first cheerful sound she'd heard in hours. His next words were even better. 'Fancy a cold drink?'

'Above diamonds,' she admitted.

'You *must* be thirsty. Here.' He passed her a can he'd retrieved from the yacht's fridge.

Nothing had ever tasted better than its sweet, fizzy but bitingly cold contents.

'You,' she told him when she felt strong enough to speak, 'have just saved my life. Again,' she added ruefully.

'I'll try not to make a habit of it. Unless of course you make it worth my while,' he said lightly. Alix had the depressing conviction that he meant it.

He stood up and, conscious of her own sweat-damp shirt, she wondered how on earth he managed to stay apparently cool and self-possessed despite the sultry heat and the crowds of the town.

When she had stowed away the foodstuff, she went on deck. Jake was doing something incomprehensible to the rigging. He looked up as she approached. 'All finished?' She nodded. 'Do you want to go ashore to look around the harbour?'

Ordinarily she'd have said yes eagerly, but the incident in town had left her feeling more drained than she would have expected; or perhaps it was just that she'd been doing too much in the powerful tropical sun. She just didn't have the energy to do anything at the moment, and shook her head. 'No, I'd rather stay here. Unless I'd be in the way,' she added hastily, seeing his quick frown.

He was watching her sharply, but she couldn't read his expression, although he always seemed to find her thoughts all too easy to follow. 'No more than usual,' he drawled laconically, and turned back to his work. Oh, well, indifference was at least better than outright hostility, especially since she was temporarily out of the energy needed for a good fight.

She picked out a book from the surprisingly wide range available and retreated to the shaded part of the deck. She never did get beyond the first chapter. When Jake shook her awake the sun was already low in the sky.

'What time is it?' she muttered automatically. It must be late.

'Nearly six. If you sleep much longer you'll be awake all night,' he told her, his voice surprisingly gentle. Where was the expected accusation of laziness?

'I'm sorry,' she apologised, trying to clear the fog from her brain. 'I'll get on with the cooking.' Was this concerned Jake part of some bizarre dream?

Apparently not. He shook his head. 'Don't worry. We can eat out if you like.'

She had planned steaks and salads. They wouldn't take long. 'No. Give me ten minutes to wake up in the shower and I'll get on with it. Have a drink or something.'

'I'll wait for you. Don't rush.'

Jake's reasonable manner and his concern for her were in their way as disturbing as his earlier rudeness. She failed to puzzle it out while she showered and changed and was still cautious when she re-entered the main cabin. The mood wouldn't last, she warned herself. Inconsistency was his only consistent feature so far.

She was wrong. He was busy in the galley when she arrived, but turned as he heard her, holding up a glass pitcher of cloudy amber liquid in which ice clinked.

'Rum punch,' he clarified. 'Have a glass before you start work.'

The long, cold, bittersweet drink with the kick of local rum in it was exactly what she needed. Nerves that even the sleep and the shower had not relaxed began to unknot.

'This,' she admitted as they sat in the cockpit watching the lights on shore brighten, 'is exactly what I needed.' Somewhere in the distance a steel band was playing.

'Glad you like the recipe. One of the locals here taught it to me years ago, swears it's the best there is—but then that's what everyone claims for their own recipe,' he chuckled.

'I think he might have been right, though.' Alix tasted the drink again. She had, like every tourist, tried rum punch at the hotel but found it both too strong and too sweet. This was perfect. 'How come you know so many people here?' she wondered carelessly and then, remembering his earlier reaction to personal questions, hurriedly added, 'I'm sorry, I——'

'It's OK,' he said. 'There's no mystery. I did a bit of work on charter boats to earn money when I was younger, then, when I could afford it, I bought my own boat. I try to come here for a month or six weeks every year.' He answered her next, unspoken question with a wry twist to his expression. 'I'm not exactly out of touch. The yacht has a very powerful radio and I've access to fax machines on most of the islands I visit. Most of the time I can be back Stateside within twenty-four hours if there's a crisis.'

'And heaven help the crisis?' Alix suggested.

'Yes. I don't take kindly to having this bit of peace and quiet disrupted.'

Especially by her. She wondered more than ever why he had even contemplated anything as intrusive as allowing her into this most private aspect of his life. But she wasn't going to ask. If there was any way to avoid dangerous territory tonight, she intended to do it.

The simple meal didn't take long to prepare and somehow the spell of the evening held. He didn't reveal any more of his private life and she said nothing of hers, but that left them an enormous field of discussion. They certainly argued about everything under the sun, but it lacked the edge of hostility and contempt that had marked most of their disagreements so far.

He caught her yawning for the second time long after they had jointly cleared away the dishes and when the only light around them came from the brilliant gleam of the stars.

'You'd better go to bed,' he ordered.

'Aye, aye, sir,' she said ironically. 'Goodnight.'

'Take care,' he warned, chuckling. 'I'm not sure they don't still flog mutineers out here.' But his 'Goodnight' was not entirely unfriendly.

She *should* have slept deeply; she was tired enough, despite the afternoon's long nap. Instead, she lay in the narrow bunk feeling uncomfortably restless and uneasy. She wanted to understand both the enigma of Jake Hunter and the confusion of her own reactions to him. He seemed to change from indifference to outright contempt for no apparent reason, and then, like tonight, he could be an easy companion whom she seemed to have known for years instead of two days.

It made no sense. Nor did her inability to switch off her own response. She might have very limited experience, but she wasn't a fool or an innocent, nor could she lie to herself about her feelings. It was just that, since the destructive affair, which had ended when her fiancé had demanded the return of his ring, she had thought that she would never again fall into that emotional trap. She had only been twenty-one at the time, but the wounds had healed very slowly and she had never forgotten the lessons she had learned. David had made it quite clear then that her only appeal had been her decorative value backed by her father's wealth, and when that had gone even her looks could not hold him. No, desire meant surrender of control, and that no longer had any place in her life, and couldn't be given one. Especially not with the man sleeping so near her to whom control was second nature.

The image of Jake sprawled naked in the warm night air in his own bunk leaped unbidden to her mind and would not be banished. Throughout yesterday's sail she had been conscious of the sleek, fit lines of his body, the broad chest and narrow hips and the muscles which moved easily beneath the bronzed skin. In the dark of her cabin she could see the jut of his chin and the aquiline line of his nose, the long, expressive mouth that could laugh or sneer with equal effect, and those light eyes which took colour from the sea and sky around him or paled to clear glass in anger. Perhaps she could have resisted all that, but it was made no easier after an evening like tonight's when, hostilities suspended—at least for a while—she had discovered a mind that was as exciting as his body.

Impatiently, Alix kicked the cotton sheet to the foot of the bunk, away from her heated body. Damn him. When she had forced her way on board his boat, the last thing she had anticipated was that she might *like* the man.

CHAPTER FOUR

A RESTLESS night meant that even a cup of coffee didn't make Alix greet the morning, or Jake, with any enthusiasm. The relentless sunshine of the tropics almost made her yearn for the familiar chill of London in winter. Somehow it seemed safer. Not that she had any intention of letting her companion know that.

'I'd better phone Bill Goddard and let him know the change of plan,' she told Jake when he asked her if she wanted to go ashore.

'You don't think he'll already have sent out alarm signals and rescue parties?' he queried. 'After all, he was expecting you back two days ago.'

Alix grimaced. 'Bill doesn't get worried until someone starts to say they can't meet a deadline.' She thought about that. 'Actually, it's not so much worried as homicidal. He'll be thrilled by my tenacity,' she added gloomily and reached for the coffee-pot.

Jake was unsympathetic. What else? 'Since you seem to have the grip of a pit bull terrier when you're after something you want, he must be permanently ecstatic,' he remarked drily.

'So what *do* I tell him?' Alix wondered irritably. Jake didn't seem disposed to be communicative about anything. She was almost glad she wasn't interviewing him. Yet.

'I thought we'd take a trip to St Bart's, and then possibly on to St Maarten.' He named the islands north of Antigua. It seemed reasonable, even interesting, until he added, 'We'll leave this evening.'

70

'*What*? But it'll be dark!' She began to wonder if he had some sort of death wish—or was it some last-minute attempt to get rid of her after all?

He sighed with ill-disguised impatience. 'It usually is at night,' he agreed.

'But——' she protested incoherently.

'Scared?' he taunted her for the second time.

Her response was automatic—the same as last time, though with less truth. 'Of course not! But why sail at night? Just to complicate matters?' she wondered.

For a moment she thought she was just going to get a bland agreement. Jake was obviously tempted to let her doubts run riot. Then he relented. 'It's a longish passage to St Bart's and I want to arrive in daylight to see what we're doing. It's not a place to approach in the dark,' he added drily, and she wondered whether he had once done exactly that.

The conversation with Bill was very much what Alix had expected: enthusiasm for her doggedness followed by a belated, and cursory, concern for her well-being. She put down the phone and rejoined Jake with a strong sense of having been abandoned by her last hope of rescue.

Back on the boat she made a casserole that could be reheated later, since she wasn't at all sure about her cooking abilities at sea. Just because she hadn't yet felt the faintest qualm of seasickness didn't mean she was going to take chances. She saw little of Jake, who disappeared into a part of the boat she knew nothing about, saying something incomprehensible about 'work on the engine'.

They left about an hour before dusk when there was still light to see by but the shadows were lengthening fast. It was strange and a little unnerving to be sailing into the fading light, although Jake obviously didn't find it unusual.

'What do we do about keeping watches?' she asked nervously. She felt safe enough steering a compass course with him beside her, but what if he wanted her to manage on her own while he slept?

'No problem. George will do most of the driving and I'll keep look-out.' His voice was dismissive.

'But what do you want me to do?' Alix protested uncertainly.

In the night, she could barely make out the shape of his face, and the profile etched against the deeper darkness of the sea was unrevealing. She saw him shrug as though it didn't matter at all what she did, and she had a sudden conviction that he regretted his invitation to sail with him. The night wasn't cold, but she shivered.

'You'd better go below and get some sleep. There's not much point in your sitting up all night.' Clearly he didn't want her up there with him. He didn't have to say that she'd only be in the way; it was obvious.

She was tempted to protest, but then it didn't seem worth it. Besides, the combination of Jake and the dark sea around them was somehow intimidating. The familiar security of her little cabin did have its appeal.

'I'll just clear away this——' she indicated the remains of the meal '—then I'll turn in.' It wasn't late, but he seemed to have left her little alternative.

'Fine.'

She suspected he had forgotten all about her almost before she had left the deck. Feeling absurdly depressed—after all, she didn't *want* another confrontation, did she?—Alix slowly prepared for bed.

She read for a while, but the book couldn't hold her attention. Eventually she switched off the light and just lay in the darkness, adjusting to the sounds around her. After the nights in harbour it was strange to be listening to the rush of water just outside the hull and the faint creak of the sails overhead. She felt safe, knowing Jake was in control, and that realisation brought a reluctant smile to her lips. 'Safe' wasn't a word she usually associated with Jake Hunter. She didn't trust anything about him—neither personally, nor in the world he represented. She had gone into financial journalism partly in order to understand the world which had destroyed her father. She had learned to be fascinated with it rather than to hate it—but nothing had persuaded her to trust it. Money and power led too easily to ruthlessness, and Jake had both. And yet here she was lying in a narrow bunk and relying on him to keep her safe. The smile twisted wryly as she drifted into a light sleep.

When she awoke she sensed several hours must have passed. The little cabin felt stuffy and she was uncomfortably hot. In harbour at least she had been able to sleep with the porthole open; now it was firmly shut. Through it, she could just glimpse the movement of the water. Something, possibly moonlight, glinted fitfully on white foam, and the water itself was obsidian-black. No... somewhere deep in it, something flickered and faded, a brief spark that was surely too bright for starshine. Excitedly, she realised it must be the phosphorescence she had read about.

Wide awake now, thoughts of the relative cool of the deck combined with the urge to see more than the small porthole allowed. Jake would be up there, of course. Would he mind? Stupid question. He'd certainly made it clear enough that he didn't want her company, but surely there was space enough for them both? Even he could hardly throw her overboard.

Repeating that conviction firmly to herself, Alix padded barefoot to the galley, her white cotton nightshirt clinging to her body in the still air. If she took him a cup of coffee he might not be too hostile. After all, he would need something to help him stay awake.

Carefully, she climbed the few steps to the deck, two mugs held gingerly in one hand. He must have heard the hatch slide open, because she saw his head turn, a darker silhouette against the general darkness.

'What the hell do you want?' he demanded roughly.

Well, she hadn't expected to be welcomed, had she? Weary irritation at his hostility made her own answer brusque. 'Nothing. I just wanted to see what night sailing was really like.' To her left, light flickered in the crest of a breaking wave. 'Is that really phosphorescence?' she asked, annoyance forgotten in wonder.

'It really is.' A sort of resigned amusement crept into his voice. 'You look like a ghost, or a schoolgirl, in that white get-up,' he noticed.

'I'm neither,' she retorted. She certainly didn't feel like either. Doubts about the wisdom of her actions were already setting in, but she couldn't—wouldn't—retreat now.

'You don't have to remind me.' His voice was very dry and then, more lightly, he wondered, 'Can you tell me why you're clutching two mugs which look as though they're about to spill any minute?'

She had almost forgotten. 'I made myself some coffee and thought you might like some. Here.' She offered a mug which he took, his fingers not touching hers. 'Can I stay?' she asked, reluctant to provoke him again but not wanting to return to the stuffiness of her cabin.

He returned his attention to the wheel. 'I suppose so. But you'd better keep back here; I don't want you falling overboard.'

Not unless he was the one to throw her. She retreated to a cushioned bench seat as far from him as possible. Gradually the magic of the night began to work its spell on her. The darkness changed everything; waves assumed shapes that could be almost anything from whales to other boats before melting away with a murmur against *Shearwater*'s side. Phosphorescence glimmered gold in the breaking foam and she and Jake might have been alone in a world with no land, no horizon, no inhabitants except a million bright stars.

Shearwater plunged confidently on into the night. 'How do you know where you're going?' she wondered aloud.

A resigned voice answered her. 'So you're still awake? You'd better have a lesson in night-driving, then. Come and take the wheel.'

Wedging her mug behind a rope and feeling very uncertain, Alix joined him. He stepped back to let her put her hands on the spokes and then closed in behind her. His free hand closed above one of hers and she was trapped between his body and the wheel. Alix's concentration wavered as she felt the brush of his chest against her back and sudden heat flooded her body. Her thin nightshirt had seemed quite adequate covering when she first came on deck. Not any more. Distracted by his nearness, she turned the wheel a little too sharply, and the yacht plunged awkwardly. His hands tightened over hers and she felt the touch of his leg against her thighs as he braced himself and corrected her mistake.

'Careful,' he warned harshly, and the warmth of his breath teased the back of her neck before he stepped away.

She would have to be *very* careful, she realised, conscious of the sudden tension coiling in her stomach. Aloud, she asked about navigation. He showed her the light which allowed her to read the compass and how to use a star to check the boat's direction. 'Why don't you use the self-steering gear?' she wondered and felt, as much as saw, the shrug of his broad shoulders.

'I like steering her myself.' He always would prefer to be in direct control, she realised. Was that part of his business success? She couldn't ask him, but another small piece fitted into the confusing and complex image she was building of him. 'Do you feel up to steering by yourself?' he asked, startling her from her thoughts. 'I want to take a quick look at the chart.'

He watched her progress for a moment and then left her. To her surprise, he didn't immediately take over again when he returned. She heard him go forward to check on the sails and then he came back, standing beside her, apparently content with the way she was coping.

He must have sensed when her concentration began to waver. 'I'll take over now,' he told her, but the sharp edge of criticism was missing. He didn't even object when she curled up on the seat instead of retreating to her cabin. The hypnotic sounds around her began to lull her into the sleep which had been elusive earlier.

A hand was on her shoulder, gently waking her. She sat up, momentarily disorientated, flinching from the tall figure looming over her. It was still dark.

'What is it?' she asked, alarmed.

He released her at once. 'Nothing to worry about.' There was wry humour in the deep voice. 'We've got company and I thought you might be interested.' He nodded towards the bow, where dark unwavelike shapes seemed to be moving, and she heard an unfamiliar splashing. 'Dolphins,' he clarified.

She scrambled to her feet in delight. 'Really? Where? Can I see?' she demanded, eager to watch creatures she had only ever read about.

'Come forward,' he said, and led the way to the yacht's bow. Absently, she realised he must have connected the self-steering gear after all. He pointed to the water. 'There.'

At first it was hard to distinguish the shapes, but as her eyes adjusted she saw there were eight of them, four on each side of the boat as if acting as an escort. They were playing in the bow-wave, she saw, coiling and diving and leaping in concert in the wave thrown up by the yacht's motion. As they dived deep she saw that phosphorescence clung to their bodies, outlining the sleek, streamlined shapes. When they broke surface she heard the gasp of their breathing and sometimes glimpsed starshine on an eye glinting up towards them as though laughingly aware of an appreciative audience. Suddenly she realised that the squeaks and clicks she was hearing had nothing at all to do with the boat's usual noises.

'I can hear them talking!' she exclaimed.

Jake too had been staring down into the water, apparently as entranced as she, but he turned at her words and she caught the lingering glint of a smile on his mouth.

'Not everyone can,' he told her. 'Most adults seem to lose the ability to hear high-pitched noises. Too many other noises in their lives, I guess.'

Remembering her own frantic city life, Alix was surprised that her own hearing had not been blunted. 'It's magical,' she told him. 'Thank you.'

He was looking at her now, and, as she searched his face, conscious of the growing tension between them, all awareness of their surroundings vanished.

'I must have been mad,' he said, his voice harsh with suppressed urgency.

Then his hands were digging into her shoulders and drawing her hard against his body, and his face blotted out even the stars. The first kiss was savage, almost angry in its intensity, parting her lips before the thought of struggle was even half formed and ravishing her mouth and senses. And then all thoughts of self-preservation were lost, drowned in the storm of desire that he unleashed in her.

One hand tightened against her waist while the other tangled in her hair, urging her head back to give greater freedom to his plundering mouth. Her own hands felt

the surprisingly soft texture of his hair against the back
of his neck and curled into the muscles of his back at
her body's reaction to the touch of his mouth against
the column of her neck.

He must have felt the tremor which ran through her.
His lips brushed her cheeks and lashes and explored the
angle of her jaw with a sudden tenderness which
weakened her utterly. If she had not been held against
him as he balanced easily with the yacht's motion, she
would have fallen.

Perhaps he sensed her weakness. He eased her down
to the deck, stretching out beside her, one arm holding
her to him in an embrace which was both protective and
possessive. Beneath her, the smooth wood of the
planking was cool, and the lift of the boat through the
waves seemed to echo the rhythm of her own cla-
mouring senses. He cupped her face, staring down at
her as though starlight might reveal all that was hidden
from him in sunlight. Above her he was a dark shape
and she could see nothing except the beginning of his
pirate's smile, but under her hands she felt the muscles
of his broad back tense and slide beneath the smooth
skin.

'Jake?' she murmured his name in sudden uncertainty, and, as though he was unable to help himself, his
mouth came down demandingly over hers, silencing her,
and she felt her body arch in helpless response.

The hand that held her hip against his slipped higher
beneath the loose fabric of her nightshirt. She felt his
fingers, strong and knowledgeable, exploring the taut
skin of her waist and flat stomach. When they moved
higher, cupping her small breast, and a teasing thumb
coaxed her nipple into aching life, she cried aloud. How
could she have guessed how much her body had needed
his touch?

The sounds she could not stifle seemed to please him. His lips were gentle on her now, touching the hollow of her neck, the curve of her shoulder where it met the nightshirt's wide neck, and lingering on the swell of her breasts. Dimly she recognised that his control was greater than hers, but the weight of his body beside her told her that his desire was as strong.

He lifted his head. 'Alix...' he muttered in a voice rough with passion and something else she could not identify. And then it was too late.

Whatever he had been going to say was lost. The yacht gave an awkward, lurching kick and she would have rolled across the deck if his sudden iron grip had not held her. A thin shower of spray scattered over them and she shivered. She heard him swear, immediately alert to his surroundings.

Cat-like, he was on his feet at once, lifting and steadying her automatically as he looked around. Ahead of them stars were being blotted out by a dark, racing line of cloud. Even she could now feel the increase in the wind's strength.

'All right?' He waited only for her quick nod before making his way back to the cockpit. She followed more cautiously. The dolphins, and the magic, were gone.

When she rejoined him he was doing something to one of the ropes. 'We're in for a squall,' he said curtly. 'We'll have to shorten sail.'

It was an order, but there was no time for courtesies, no time yet even to think about what had just happened between them. They worked together to change the heavy sails as the wind increased violently, the darkness and the urgency making Alix clumsy.

White water flung itself over the yacht's side, snatching at her bare feet before rushing away down the deck. She slipped. Jake's hand grabbed her arm and held her with bruising strength against the pull of wind and sea and

then released her as they both turned again to what had
to be done. No time even for a quick word of thanks
which, anyway, would not have been heard over the
scream of the wind.

Against the power of the storm there was nothing they
could do except run with the wind, off their chosen
course, and wait for the dawn. Jake fought the wheel
to keep *Shearwater* under some sort of control and Alix
crouched in the cockpit beside him, battered almost to
numbness by the constant noise and buffeting of the
wind. At his shouted command she had managed to find
oilskin jackets and safety harnesses for them both, but
she had refused to take refuge below. The nightmare was
worse down there with the boat lurching unpredictably
and the air damp and stifling. The fear of being trapped
if the yacht capsized was far worse than the discomfort
of being in the open. Besides, while she could see Jake
at the wheel, something in Alix refused to believe that
the storm would win.

Shearwater plunged on through mounting seas, sometimes shuddering when an erratic wave hit her unexpectedly, making her hesitate, before the wind drove her
mercilessly on. They had only one small sail up now and
a cold, driving rain added to the night's miseries,
numbing mind as well as body.

Alix looked up and realised that there was nothing
insensible about Jake. He was watching sea and sky with
fierce concentration, but she also saw the quick glint of
an exultant grin and realised that he was actually enjoying the challenge thrown down by nature. Irrationally,
her own spirits lifted and she smiled.

He must have caught some movement, because he
glanced over at her and laughed aloud. Even in the half-
light of pre-dawn, she thought she could see the devils
dancing in his blue eyes. At that moment he might have
been some victorious corsair, glorying in the adventure

of the storm. Her own heart beat faster in response and she found herself, suddenly warmed, laughing back at him. For a moment, fear was submerged in exhilaration.

A grey dawn eventually began to creep in, revealing no obvious break in the fury of the weather. Alix felt beyond fear or exhaustion now and could hardly understand the strength which was keeping Jake alert at the wheel. She stared at the confusion of sea around them and wondered when it would ever end. Then she realised that ahead was something that was not being driven by the force of the wind. Land. Safety. Feeling a surge of relief, she tugged urgently at Jake's arm, and he followed her pointing finger.

His sudden oath and the tightening of his expression were all she needed to tell her that her relief was misplaced. His face was grim, all exultation gone. She watched him, uncertain of the danger, but convinced of its reality. He was fighting the storm now, not running with it, trying to force the boat away from the nearing landmass. Moment by moment she thought he would succeed, her own nails digging into her palms as the immediate peril of their situation became dramatically clear as they inched towards safety.

A clatter from the sail and an abrupt, lurching halt to *Shearwater*'s progress altered everything.

'You'll have to hold her,' Jake shouted, and barely waited for her to take over from him before scrambling, cat-like, to the useless sail. Beneath her hands the wheel kicked and struggled like some panic-stricken creature and Alix watched without understanding as Jake fought the flapping canvas.

When he came back to the cockpit the sail was functioning again, but even her inexperienced eye could tell that all was far from well. Jake's expression was bleak as he took the wheel from her.

'We won't clear the land. If it's where I think it is, there's one possible anchorage. We'll have to try for it or we'll pile up on the reef.' Ahead, Alix could already see waves breaking white over the hidden danger. 'If we hit, get away from the boat as fast as you can and try not to get too cut up on the coral. Go and put on some jeans.'

She couldn't move. Anger, as well as fear, held her rigid. Fate had cheated both Jake and herself, but they would at least face this together. The roar of the surf was loud now, even over the sound of the wind, and destruction seemed inevitable. Why try to avoid a few cuts? *Nothing* could live in that maelstrom. Jake must have realised it too, because he didn't repeat his command, his whole concentration focused on the impossibly narrow gap that he must have seen earlier but which Alix had only just picked out.

How he did it she would never know. When the moment of impact seemed inevitable and the sea was breaking all around them, *Shearwater* flew like a dart at the gap, seemed almost to hesitate, and then surfed through the white water into the comparative calm of the lagoon beyond.

After that it was merely a matter of limping slowly towards the cove that Jake indicated, dropping the anchor, and letting the torn sail collapse in a crumpled heap on the deck. All Alix wanted to do was imitate it. The sudden silence, and the reprieve from the battering of the past hours was almost unbearable.

Jake looked around at the small cove. His expression was still grim. When he turned to Alix, she saw that his eyes were bloodshot and that salt was drying on his face. Her own skin felt tight and raw.

'Are we safe?' She needed to hear it confirmed.

Jake nodded. 'Safe enough.' He surveyed the chaos on the decks. 'We'll sort this mess out later. What we both need now is a shower and some sleep.'

She couldn't argue with that, although there was something about the way he said 'this mess' which made her wonder exactly what he meant. Besides the obvious.

Neither remembered fear nor remembered passion could have kept Alix awake long. When, however, she awoke, aware that the day was well advanced and that Jake was moving around the deck above her head, she lay for a long time replaying the incident that the storm had interrupted. It was what she had feared might happen, though nothing in her experience or imagination had prepared her for the uncontrolled fire of passion between them. Only the storm around them could have stopped the storm between them. A few minutes later and she wasn't convinced even that would have stopped them. But that didn't make it right. Safe at anchor, though heaven—and Jake—knew where, she knew that she had to leave soon. If she stayed, it might happen again—and desire without love could only be disastrous. Most of the time Jake despised her, and she hardly knew who he really was. No. She must go back to her familiar world where men were colleagues and desire was something grown out of long ago and there was nothing the senses wanted that overrode the reasoned arguments of the mind. And where Jake Hunter was nothing more than a corporate raider whose exploits helped sell newspapers.

On deck, Jake had already tidied away most of the confusion from last night and the planking was already drying out, stained with the white tide marks of salt. All the hatches were open wide to air out the yacht, and Alix was surprised at how little evidence remained of last night's battering. Hands on hips, head tilted back, Jake was staring up at the length of the mast. He must have heard her approach because he turned quickly, watching her with an expression which was almost cautious.

'Are you OK? Not too many bruises?' The words sounded concerned enough, but there was a detachment in his voice. So he, too, had decided to draw back from what had happened. Alix could almost see the 'No Trespassing' sign. She should be both pleased and relieved; this odd feeling of hurt was ridiculous. He was still watching her, and clearly wanted an answer. She shook her head.

'No. I'm fine.' A sudden uneasy laugh shook her voice. 'After those last few minutes coming through the reef, I think I'd consider myself fine with two broken legs. I don't know how you did it.'

'Luck.' She wanted to protest against the dismissive tone which rejected any compliment to his skill, but the expression on his face stopped her.

She looked around her instead. '*Shearwater* isn't much damaged, is she?' In the space of a few days she had come to care about the lovely yacht and knew that his feelings ran far deeper.

'Most of it's superficial,' he agreed. 'A bit of paint and varnish gone, a couple of minor fittings bent or loosened.'

That sounded great, so why was he still frowning, and what had been the implied reservation in that last statement? '*Most* of it...?' she repeated, hearing again the faint emphasis he had used.

His lips twisted in a humourless smile. 'Look up there.' Her eyes followed the finger which pointed up the mast. At first, in the mass of wire, she could distinguish nothing. Then she saw that, amid all its tight symmetry, one piece hung loose and twisting with the boat's slight motion. She looked a query.

'That's why the foresail collapsed,' he explained. 'That bit of rigging parted under the strain. And we can't go anywhere till I've replaced it. The strain on the mast would be too much if we tried to hoist a sail without it.'

She took his word for it, and looked around their anchorage. There were no obvious signs of other people. A hundred yards away a wide, sandy beach fringed with green bushes ran down to the sea; the water was clear and inviting and she thought she had seldom seem a more idyllic anchorage. Another few hours' delay, possibly another night on board, could surely do no harm?

'Will it take long to get the parts?' she wondered. Perhaps that accounted for his concern.

'No, I've all I need on board. The rigging won't take much more than a day or two. After that I'll have to check and possibly refasten a few of the hull's seams. After the pounding she took last night I can't afford to take it for granted that they're still watertight. Then I'll have a go at the engine.'

'The...?' The list of problems was growing longer by the minute. And so was the time-scale.

'You remember I had a look at it in Antigua?' She nodded. She had assumed he had just been avoiding her. 'Well, it's been giving trouble all season. I finally located the problem then and it's obvious that the engine's taking us nowhere without a lot of work. I was planning to get an engineer to look at it in St Bart's,' he added ruefully.

'Isn't there someone here who could do it? I mean, a bit more quickly than you could,' Alix explained hastily when his eyes narrowed on her in surprise. She hadn't *meant* to insult his mechanical ability, so why was he looking at her like that? She looked around again. 'How far is the nearest town?'

His harsh laugh held very little amusement. She stared up at the flat, unyielding planes of his face, wondering what on earth she had said.

The laughter died and there was grim satisfaction in his voice when he said, 'This islet isn't even big enough to have a name on the chart. You could walk across it in half an hour and, until we arrived, its only inhabitants were a few rats and several hundred birds. You're marooned on a tropical island, lady, and you won't be going anywhere else at all for at least a week.'

SLOWLY, Alix stared around again. What she had taken to be a peninsula of the main island was in fact all there was. Their little cove was probably its only beach. Now she really looked, she began to see that what they were on was just a palm-covered lump of coral in the middle of the lagoon.

'One day it might grow up into a proper tourist resort,' Jake drawled, obviously following her growing panic with no trouble at all. 'For the moment, though, it's just the two of us.'

Just the two of us. Every romantic cliché in the world seemed to hang mockingly on that phrase. Hysteria wasn't far away, but *someone* had to find a way out of 'this mess'. And now she knew exactly what he had meant by those words.

She had a moment's inspiration. 'The radio?' she asked eagerly, but he was already shaking his head.

'The aerial went in the storm. It's useless.'

'But I'm due back in the office!' Even she could hear how absurd the desperate plea must sound. Never had civilisation, with all its problems, seemed more remote. Or appealing. And never had she been more acutely aware of the piratical qualities of Jake Hunter aboard his own yacht.

'And my people are expecting to hear from me,' he agreed softly. 'It won't do them any harm to worry a little, and anyway, it's too bad; they'll just have to sweat it out. And so, Alix,' he added, his eyes never leaving hers, 'will you.'

When he said 'sweat', she realised ruefully a few hours later, he meant it quite literally. After his words she had wanted to turn and run, seized by a primitive reaction that urged her to escape while she still had a chance. But there was nowhere to run and her last chance of rescue had been blown away in the storm. Besides, she told herself sternly, whatever their surroundings, they *weren't* primitive, just two people from the civilised modern world caught up in a purely temporary problem. Looking at the rakish tilt to Jake's jaw as he watched her and the sardonic smile which told her he had read the panic-stricken impulse on her expressive face, Alix hadn't quite convinced herself. As ever, her response had been to meet challenge with challenge.

'Where do I start?' she had asked. It was a question she was to regret. If sailing had damaged the occasional fingernail, the work that she was now involved in made her understand just how Jake had acquired the calluses on his hands. They wrestled stubborn, greasy coils of wire from deep within the yacht's lockers and fought to measure and straighten it. When Jake went up the mast to remove the damaged rigging, Alix had to help on the winch, and he seemed to need her assistance in every awkward and dirty stage of the job.

By the time he decided that they had done enough for the day she was beyond caring about the risks of another night in his company. All she wanted was a long swim to cool off and stretch her aching muscles.

The warm salt water was certainly soothing. She swam slowly towards the beach, enjoying the smooth flow of the water against her body. She had no towel, but she had noticed a flat rock just above the water-line, and she could sit there and absorb the evening sun. She began to walk ashore through the softly rippling waves which were such a contrast with last night's breakers. The sand beneath her feet was warm from the day's heat. Last night's brush with disaster seemed to have sharpened all her senses, making her freshly aware of the textures and colours of the simplest things. Especially, she thought ruefully, of the pleasure of having solid ground beneath her feet. She turned to look back at the yacht and saw Jake moving round on deck. Then he straightened and poised for a moment on the boat's side before knifing into a shallow racing dive that sent him arcing across the water and into it with scarcely a splash.

The after-image of that perfect body in a moment of near-flight stayed with Alix as she watched him cut through the clear water in a fast and efficient crawl. But she had no intention of being caught staring, and she was lying on the large rock with her eyes closed in apparent relaxation when he walked ashore.

A shower of water drops disturbed her. She sat up, spluttering and indignant. 'Blast you!'

'Quite,' he accepted cheerfully. 'Don't you know it's dangerous to sleep in the sun?'

'I wasn't asleep,' she said honestly, with what dignity she could.

'Could've fooled me,' he commented. 'Move over; you're hogging the best seat on the beach.'

It seemed safer not to argue. She shifted to the far side of the rock and he sprawled beside her. The rock wasn't quite as large as it had first seemed.

She looked seaward. She had seen him dressed like this from their first meeting; there was no reason at all for her eyes to linger on the way beads of water glistened against his chest and the wet shorts dragged against his flat stomach.

'I suppose there must be worse places to be marooned,' she said at last, needing to break the silence. And she was right; the pale blue sea, darkening suddenly to cobalt beyond the line of the reef, with the graceful white yacht riding peacefully at anchor, was straight out of someone's dream of the Caribbean. Even knowing they were stuck here had some benefits. Suddenly deadlines and telephones and Stock Exchange gossip were all beyond her reach, and there was something strangely liberating about the knowledge.

'We're lucky.' She wasn't sure if Jake's words echoed what she was seeing or was a comment on their safety after the gale. Perhaps both. He was right, after all.

She didn't want to talk about the work left to do, or speculate on when they'd be able to leave. It was too peaceful sitting here, watching the sun slipping into the horizon beyond the sea. A glance at Jake showed that he too was absorbed by the simple beauty of the scene. Unfortunately, a single glance wasn't quite enough. The dying sunlight cast his body in bronze and shadows. She swallowed, suddenly aware of her own body's tightening and the contrasts between her smooth legs and the powerful hair-roughened thighs of the man only inches away from her.

She looked up and found her own gaze snared in the sea-blue of his. Something flared between them, like the raw fire of the setting sun, and then Jake was standing up, stretching, and she couldn't see his face.

'We don't want to be caught out here in the dark.' His voice was light, a thread of something that might have been laughter, or something else, running through it. 'Race you back to the boat. Last one aboard cooks the dinner!'

He had hit the water in a low, running dive even before she had got to her feet. Not that it would have been much of a race anyway, she acknowledged, and at least it dispelled the web of tension that had been momentarily spun between them.

When she at last reached *Shearwater*'s side he reached down a strong hand from the deck and, grinning in triumph, helped haul her on board.

'I had every intention of cooking anyway,' Alix said honestly, managing to suggest injured dignity at the same time, before her own chuckle mingled amicably with his.

That seemed to set the tone for the rest of the evening, and there was no repetition of that uncomfortable awareness either then or through the next day's hard work. It was strange how quickly a routine could become established, Alix reflected: work, a swim to watch the sunset from the shore, lingering over a simple meal on deck by the light of a single lamp. Those first three days had a curiously dream-like unreality; it even seemed as though she and Jake had arrived at some sort of truce where, as long as they avoided personal issues, they could actually enjoy each other's company. She hardly thought about the world waiting for them beyond the reef.

It was Jake who broke the unwritten rules. On the third evening they were sitting late over the remains of their meal when he said, out of nowhere, 'Why aren't you married?'

At least the deep shadows hid her jolt of surprise and the sudden moment of calculation as she debated what to say. Jake had been good company recently, but a pirate off duty was still a pirate, and you didn't knowingly invite one on to your private territory.

'Don't tell me you haven't had any offers,' he insisted, clearly determined on an answer. 'Not with looks like yours.'

It wasn't a compliment she cherished. Oddly enough, she didn't even think of telling him to mind his own business. Not that it would have worked; he'd made his fortune through other people's business, after all.

Alix looked down at her empty wine glass and out into the darkness of the night and the blacker darkness of her own past. 'I was engaged once,' she admitted with an attempt at lightness. 'It didn't work out.'

'Why not?' A harsh note she hadn't heard in days was in his voice. 'Wasn't he rich enough?'

The irony of that made her smile wryly. If only he knew; the truth was entirely the other way round. But she wasn't going to tell him of the humiliation of David's retreat as soon as he heard of her father's bankruptcy.

'He wanted a doormat and I decided not to be one,' she told him instead, with forced lightness. Looking back, she could see that it was true in a way. If she had married as a very naïve and immature twenty-one-year-old, she would never have thought of pursuing her own career. On the whole, she had gained more than she had lost. David had certainly not been worth all the humiliated and heart-broken tears she had shed, but perhaps he had done her a favour after all. It was an oddly liberating thought which had never before occurred to her. Jake's response, however, shattered any momentary pleasure she might have felt.

'So you gave the poor guy the shove because he wasn't much use to you?' He stood up abruptly, pushing back from the table.

His height dominated the limited space of the saloon, and it was only the habit of defiance that stopped Alix from flinching back in her seat. Hit back before he can really hurt you, she told herself, reacting to the sudden return of contempt she heard in his voice.

'At least I didn't marry him and then dump him as soon as he looked like being as successful as me,' she retorted, deliberately ignoring the knowledge that Ellen Carter's career had only really taken off after her divorce.

For one moment she thought he was going to shake her, or worse. His very stillness after he had turned swiftly towards her was frightening. Then he said softly, 'As soon as I saw you lying on the beach in that flimsy shirt, I should have known that that was exactly the sort of "success" you admired.' He laughed, but there was no humour at all in the sound. 'You're a lot cleverer than Ellen, but underneath you're as cold and ambitious as she was, and I'll bet you know even better than she did how to use men to get what you want. *You* don't even bother to pretend that commitments like marriage have any value.'

The sheer depth of his disgust was shocking. His image of her both repelled and angered Alix. She slipped from her seat, facing him to reject everything he accused her of. 'You don't know the first thing about me,' she told him, hearing her voice shake with the effort of control. 'The sooner you can get this boat ready for sea again, the better. You've misjudged me from the moment we met and I don't care. If I value anything, it's certainly not *your* opinion!'

Thank heaven her own cabin was just behind her. She was able to slip in there and shut the door firmly behind her, leaning back against it and breathing hard as though she had been in a fight.

Unfortunately, she wasn't able to shut out his final mocking comment before she heard him walk away. 'That's not what you thought on the night of the storm.'

How *dared* he remind her of those crazy moments of passion when he had spent so much time ignoring them? It wasn't as though she needed reminding, she reflected ruefully as she climbed reluctantly into her bunk. It was too early for bed really, but she had no wish to risk another encounter with Jake yet, and he had certainly given her plenty to think about. She wondered why he had brought the subject of marriage up. Did he *want* an excuse to quarrel with her? Absurd. And just what had his wife done to make him react like that? It had certainly seemed as though Jake was making Alix pay for something Ellen Carter had done. Surely she couldn't have been unfaithful? It didn't take any effort at all to conjure up an image of Jake's lean and powerful body, and she had an overwhelming, if brief taste of his sensual power, so that the thought of someone rejecting him was clearly ridiculous. Besides, there must be plenty of other willing women around if he needed reassurance. He probably had blonde bimbos stacked seven deep back in the States, she thought with unusual acidity, and shifted uncomfortably in bed, wishing he hadn't reminded her of those moments in his arms.

Perhaps it was just her age. At twenty-seven her body was probably just telling her she shouldn't be living like a nun. Too bad. She had managed perfectly well up to now and, if she had had any doubts about the wisdom of avoiding emotional entanglements, the present situation certainly ought to put her straight. Look what had just happened. She turned over again, the cotton sheet wrinkling uncomfortably beneath her. Desire, or whatever this irrational response was, would just have to take second place to common sense. It was an admirable resolution, but somehow it failed to soothe her into an untroubled sleep.

The atmosphere next morning was tense, and Alix realised that Jake was being almost as careful as she was to avoid trouble. Somehow, that irritated her, so that when he said, 'You've done a good job there,' as he looked at the sail she'd been mending, something snapped.

'Even though I'm a woman?'

He seemed taken aback. 'What's that got to do with it? Not many jobs on a boat need brute strength. There are plenty of first-class women sailors.'

That wasn't what she had meant. 'So what have you got against women journalists?' she wondered aloud, more bluntly than she'd intended, with a sense of burning her boats.

His eyes narrowed. 'Not much, although I don't think much of most of the junk they turn out.' Alix thought of the magazine she'd been reading when they first met. 'In fact,' he went on deliberately, 'I've nothing against women in any career they choose to take on. Several directors in my companies are women—all I care about is how well they do the job.' He stared at her. Despite the warmth of the day his eyes were cold, and he leaned back against the rigging, surveying her in a way which reminded her of that first interview. 'Or are you wondering what exactly I have against *you*?' he asked, the drawl both soft and menacing.

'Yes, I was wondering exactly that,' Alix admitted defiantly. She was fed up with fighting his unpredictable moods and unreasonable hostility. It would be better to know exactly what she was supposed to have done to make him look at her with such scorn. At least then she could either sort things out or ignore him. If that last seemed unlikely, that was her business. So what did he dislike so much about her? At the moment he was looking as though there was so much that he hardly knew where to start.

'What I despise more than anything else,' he said flatly, 'is the sort of female dishonesty that makes a woman like you prefer to use her body rather than her brain to get what she wants.'

He might as well have slapped her. 'What on earth do you mean?' she managed when she could say anything. 'If you're talking about the other night——'

He interrupted before she could mention those minutes of passion before the storm had broken. Besides, his contempt had been evident long before then. 'Not that.' He dismissed it as though it had meant nothing. 'I mean people who dress in revealing clothes but shriek if someone touches them—unless they want something. I mean that first morning when you lay around on the beach waiting for me and then flirted oh, so prettily to get my attention. By the time you "discovered" who I was,' he sneered, 'I suppose you expected me to be so overwhelmed by your charms that I'd give you the interview and then we could spend the next few days indulging our mutual passion? You certainly chased after me hard enough.'

Alix *did* hit him. She felt the sting in her palm before she had even begun to realise what she intended, but there was no room for second thoughts in the white-hot rage that consumed her. It didn't even matter that he looked more than ready to retaliate.

'You conceited, pigheaded *oaf*,' she shouted at him. 'So you think anyone on a beach you happen to appear on must be in pursuit of you? Well, you can think again. I wanted the interview with you because it's part of my job, but I'd rather never see another word of mine in print than do what you're suggesting. I'm surprised you ever let me on your precious boat if that's what you believe I'm capable of. Are you really so preoccupied with power and money that you think that's all that turns women on?'

His mouth was a thin line edged with white, and the print of her hand stood out red against his cheek. After the first convulsive move towards her when she struck him he had stayed rigidly still, but she could see the banked fury in his eyes and the control with which he gripped a wire stay.

'Anyone who's been poor values money,' he retorted. 'But you wouldn't even begin to know anything about that.'

'Oh, I know what poverty is,' she told him, almost beyond caring now what she revealed about herself, but he was hardly listening.

'Oh, yeah? Like not being able to afford another silk shirt?' he sneered. 'Don't tell me you didn't have rich parents and weren't brought up with every possible luxury. It shows every time you move and in everything you say.'

In other circumstances, she thought with a ridiculous urge to laugh at the irony of his words, that might have been a compliment. Not now. The contempt in his open appraisal of her, vulnerable in only a swimsuit and shirt, stung. She lifted her chin. Even if she had been willing to lie, she had no intention of even trying to defend herself. And she certainly wouldn't tell him the truth.

'Yes, my parents had money,' she said coolly. And so what? was her unspoken, but obvious, addition. No need to tell him of the financial crash that had led to her father's ruin and suicide, not to mention David's defection, and her need to support herself. 'As for the rest,' she added, her voice as dismissive as his had ever been, 'I don't care what you think. I've told you that I had no idea what the great Jake Hunter looked like before we met, and, if you choose to believe your own paranoia, then it's your problem and you can deal with it. Meanwhile,' she added, stooping swiftly to pick up her book and towel and the hat she wore to shade herself against the sun, 'I'm going ashore. I don't want any company and if there's something you want fixed on your wretched boat you can damn well fix it yourself!'

She turned and climbed down into the dinghy, her hands fumbling to untie its mooring line. Her efforts at paddling the little boat were clumsy and badly coordinated and Jake could have stopped her easily, but he made no move to do so. She could feel him still staring at her from the boat as she hauled the dinghy up on to the sand and walked off down the beach, but she was not going to look back.

It was only when she reached the narrow far end of the beach, where the green bushes grew close to the shore and she could get no further away from the boat, that she realised her hands were shaking. Awkwardly, she spread out the big towel and lay down as though sun-bathing. Here, even through binoculars, he could not see the stream of tears that coursed down her face as the devastating scene replayed itself mockingly.

How could he have believed she could behave like that? Would anyone? Reluctantly she conceded they would; there were people in her profession who would do what he had suggested. But not working on papers as pres-tigious as hers, nor would she or most of her colleagues even really call them journalists. And that wasn't the point. That he could still think it after the past few days meant that he didn't know anything at all about her and that nothing they had shared meant anything, not even those dizzying moments in the darkness before the storm.

She had begun to think they were developing some sort of understanding; now she could only be more glad than ever that things had gone no further between them that night. That would surely have confirmed every sus-picion he already had about her. What had made a man like Jake who had so many fine qualities—sensitivity, intelligence, humour—so cynical about women? Clearly it wasn't, despite what she had thought, their pro-fessional ambitions he objected to. No, this was far more personal, as though no woman could want him for himself. Which had to be ridiculous. She had only to shut her eyes and his tall, bronzed body with its uncon-scious grace, the aquiline face with the smile that could widen into a grin of delight or turn lop-sided in amused mockery, was before her. Even in her anger and distress she could feel her own response to the image she could conjure so treacherously easily. Was it really his mar-riage that had made him so hostile? Despite herself she could almost pity him for the damage that had been done to him.

About the damage to herself she could hardly bear to think yet. It had taken that flaring argument and her own reactions to his accusations for her to realise just how much more was involved than physical attraction, although that on its own was frighteningly strong. No, some time among all the arguments and hostility of the week they had been together something else had grown. Not love. It couldn't be that. Alix shrank from both the word and the thought. But there was some feeling for the man she had glimpsed from time to time, particularly recently, behind the defences he had built.

So she had been with Jake Hunter for a week. She clearly wasn't going to get the interview, she acknowledged, a rueful and watery smile touching her lips. Unfortunately she had no idea how much longer it would be before Jake decided *Shearwater* was safe to sail in. At least, after this morning's scene, he must be in as much of a hurry as she was.

She sat up, looking around at the little bay. In other circumstances she would have thought it an enchanted spot; now it was a trap. She could imagine the comments of her colleagues back at work if they heard about her being alone on a tropical island with a good-looking man, and decided she would be saying very little about it to them. By now, though, Bill would be expecting to hear from her. Despite herself she smiled at the thought of his growing irritation when she didn't contact him and his expression—and language—as he realised that you couldn't simply telephone a yacht. At what stage, if at all, would concern for a god-daughter take over from an editor's anger with a journalist who missed a deadline? Alix wasn't at all sure, but she would presumably find out in the next few days.

The most immediate problem was those few days themselves. Sooner or later she was going to have to go back on board. Jake would probably either say something sarcastic or pretend nothing had ever happened and retreat behind his mask of indifference. That would

be the easiest situation to cope with, but she wasn't sure
she could trust herself not to make one more attempt to
convince him he was wrong about her—despite the inevitable humiliation which would follow.

She stood up, suddenly restless. After all, she had faced
worse than this before. At twenty-one it had been her
whole life that had collapsed in ruins overnight. This
was surely nothing so dramatic, just a clash of person-
alities and a rather unpleasant end to a doomed assignment. Put like that, it was nothing. Moodily, she
kicked the dry sand just above the water-line. She wasn't
even convincing herself.

She didn't feel like swimming and she certainly wasn't
going to walk back down the beach towards the dinghy,
and the yacht. She didn't even want to look in that direction. Jake was probably working away at something
on board as though nothing had happened, and she
would rather not see that. It seemed like a good idea to
explore the little bit of land there was on the islet, but
a step or two reminded her that she wouldn't get far
without shoes. Her book lay discarded on the towel. At
least if she looked as though she were reading she might
appear to be enjoying herself. If anyone happened to
look. But she was too agitated to settle down. She wandered over to the mass of lush green bushes.

They were covered in small fruit, like green tomatoes
or unripe apples. Unconsciously she reached out to touch
a cluster hanging low on a nearby branch.

'Don't touch it!' The whipcrack of command in Jake's
voice whirled her round.

'Why not? What's wrong? What do you think——?'
What was he doing here? How had he got here so quietly?
And why? Couldn't he leave her alone for a few hours?
Belatedly, anger began to surface.

He took two quick strides towards her, ignoring her
protest and her automatic half-step backwards. With

almost cruel force he seized her wrists, holding her hands palm upwards, away from her body. Fierce blue eyes stared into hers, a frown driving a deep crease between his brows.

'Did you touch anything?' he demanded, his voice still urgent.

'No.' Alix tugged hard, but failed to free herself. 'Let me go!' There was an edge of panic in her voice now. She didn't know what was wrong; she didn't recognise or understand this mood, but she didn't like it. He kept his grip on her wrists, but it eased slightly, although she knew she couldn't break free.

'Are you sure you didn't even touch the leaves?' His eyes held hers, demanding an answer.

She thought about it, since it seemed so important, but shook her head. 'No.' His shout had stopped her. 'Why? Is it some rare and endangered species?' she wondered, looking eloquently at the flourishing bushes which seemed to run riot over most of the island.

'Hardly.' His voice was dry, as though he could afford to be annoyed now that he knew she had touched nothing. 'Didn't anyone warn you about manchineel bushes?'

'About...? Oh, yes.' She vaguely remembered a leaflet in her hotel room which had cautioned tourists against the few local dangers. But the beach had been cleared of them; these were the first she had seen. 'Is that what this stuff is?' She looked again at the deceptively innocuous shrub.

His lips tightened. 'Yes. Even touching the leaves can give you a nasty rash, and the fruit could land you in a hospital for a week. Or worse,' he told her flatly, adding, 'The locals swear that just sleeping in its shade will make you ill.'

'Will it?' It didn't seem possible.

'I don't know. I've never felt very keen to find out. And I don't advise you to try.'

She shuddered at how easily she might have hurt herself—with no chance of getting to a doctor. 'I suppose I really ought to thank you this time,' she said reluctantly, suddenly aware that his hands still held her wrists.

He looked down at them and then back up to her face. Something in his expression made her try to draw back against his tightening clasp.

She heard a sound like a shaken laugh and then he muttered, 'I can think of a way,' and pulled her fully into a hard embrace.

CHAPTER SIX

ALIX'S immediate reaction was to struggle. 'No!' This wasn't what she wanted. Not here. Not now. Not in anger, with nothing resolved between them. But she might as well not have spoken, and there was never a chance that she would escape his embrace if he chose to compel her. His hand cupping her head urged it back so that her lips were his for the taking.

She tried to brace herself, pushing against the warm flesh of his shoulders, but he only drew her more tightly against his hips, and she felt his urgent arousal. When he lifted his head, staring down into her wide, dark eyes, his own blazing with anger and desire, she thought for one moment he would set her free. But something, a look almost of desperation or pain, flickered momentarily in his face and he bent his head towards hers again. When she fought harder he clipped both her hands behind her back in one of his, arching her body yet closer.

Her only defence was stillness. As his mouth closed over hers she tried to stay impassive, to ignore the heat of his body, still damp from his swim to the shore, against hers. But then the hand against her head moved lower, brushing against her bare shoulders, and she realised that the halter strap of her swimsuit was loose. Then his hand was against her breast and her involuntary gasp was all he needed to gain entry to her mouth.

Need. It was all she could feel—his need, which was permitting no denial and her own, rigidly suppressed, which was beginning to clamour at her self-control.

Strangely enough, she felt no fear. When the hands that held her so fiercely slackened their hold and the touch of his lips gentled, teasing and coaxing a response from her, she could not contain the tiny moan that caught in her throat. Without her willing it, her arms were round his neck now, holding him close when he would, at last, have released her. Her own body was betraying her now, and he knew it.

With a shaken laugh that had an edge of triumph in it, he drew her down with him to the towel on the sand. Again she felt the urgency of his lips against hers, as though he could not satisfy his need to taste her. And her own hunger for him rose to meet his demand. All the tension, all the aggression, all the hostility that had raged between them burned in a fury of passion that denied either resistance or analysis. His hands stripped away her costume, then he lifted away from her and was suddenly still, his eyes lingering on what he had revealed. With a sense of awe she realised that the hand he lifted to cup her small breast was shaking.

'You are quite perfect,' he said quietly and, bending, took her into his mouth. She could not control the electric response that surged through her, and her cry of pleasure echoed in the sunlight like the far-off cry of a gull as he caressed both her breasts before returning to her mouth. What had once seemed inadequate to her became the essence of femininity under the touch of his lips and the roving exploration of his hands.

All the savagery of those first few minutes had gone, and Alix now was as urgent as Jake for what she had been denying since their first meeting. Her body felt boneless beneath the touch of his knowing fingers, which conspired to make her gasp with pleasure as they traced the line of her waist, then caressed the golden colour of her thighs and lingered on the smooth whiteness above, where her flesh was untanned. Beneath the intimacy of his questing hands she felt something deep within her melt and blossom.

But she did not want simply to surrender to his skill. Suddenly she needed to explore the tanned body which had entranced her since she had first seen him. Pushing lightly at the shoulders above her, she felt him lift his mouth from its investigation of the delicate line of her collarbone. His eyes, warm now with a light she had never seen before—the fire of passion tempered by something which might almost have been tenderness—scanned her face with understanding as he let her urge him back on to the towel.

She brushed light kisses over his face, exploring by taste and touch what had become familiar to her sight: the broad forehead, the long fair lashes and the fine creases at the corners of his eyes where he narrowed them against the sunlight. Beneath her lips she discovered the soft vulnerability of his throat and teased the fullness of his lower lip with her tongue, her own excitement rising as she felt the effect she was having on him.

'Witch!' he growled, tracing the long line of her back so that she shivered and pressed closer to him.

His body was bronze and iron beneath her hands. The fine scattering of hair on his chest was familiar to her, but only now did she have the freedom she had wanted to touch it with hands and lips, following its path from the breadth of his chest as it narrowed to the taut muscles of his waist.

A strong hand against the back of her head held her motionless. She sensed the control he was suddenly having to use, and hesitated.

'Hold still.' His voice was uneven. 'I can't take much more of that.'

She wasn't sure how much longer the demands of her own body could be denied. It had already shown her age-old knowledge and a sensuality she had not known she possessed; now need was becoming imperative. The hand against the back of her neck was gentle now, caressing. She realised he was undoing the long plait of her hair, unwinding each strand as though it were somehow precious until it was spread like a shawl across her back. Then his hands were tangling in its rich, dark mass, lifting her face to his, and any control she might have had left her. She gasped as he moved suddenly and she found herself lying beneath him once more.

It was almost as though he was taking tender revenge for her effect on him. His mouth provoked and taunted till she gasped for mercy and murmured in complaint when he did hold back. When his kisses travelled all over her body with an intimacy which was wholly new to her, she stiffened momentarily with surprise before surrendering helplessly to the unfamiliar, wild sensations he was arousing in her.

He seemed to know her body better than she did herself. Wave after wave of mounting sensation swept her towards something she had never known. Almost in fear, her hands tightened on his shoulders, and he lifted his head, understanding as well as passion in his eyes as he gathered her closer, mastering her body in one fluid movement.

He must have heard her slight gasp as his strength filled her, because he was immediately still, one hand gently brushing the hair back from her forehead as he watched her face.

'It's all right,' he told her, his voice soothing, and the quick flare of panic died as he moved slowly, and then urgently, against her, and all the suppressed fires flared up to consume them both.

It could have been minutes or hours later before she felt him lift his body from her. She murmured in protest at the sudden loss, trying to tighten her lax clasp on the sweat-slick muscles of his back, but he chuckled lazily and turned on his side, drawing her against him in a gentle embrace.

'I don't want to crush you,' he explained, and, content that he was not leaving her, she let herself drift in a weightless dream.

When she opened her eyes, unsure how much time had passed, he was propped on one elbow, watching her, tenderness and a faint question in his expression.

'Are you OK?' he asked searchingly.

'I think so.' How could she know? She had never felt like this before, never given herself to any man with such total abandon. The memory of what they had done was suddenly too much to cope with. She sat up, clasping her arms around her knees defensively, not looking at his nakedness. Soft as a falling leaf, she felt his hand come up to touch the cascade of her hair, and then it fell back before she could respond, and he was standing, reaching for his shorts.

'It's getting late; we'd better go back.' His voice was gentle, but she shivered, wrapping the towel awkwardly around her, the crumpled swimsuit clutched in one hand. He took it from her, keeping hold of her hand as they walked in silence back to the dinghy.

They said nothing until they were back on the yacht, but, as he helped Alix back on board, Jake's eyes looked keenly down into hers. 'Regrets?' he asked softly.

She shook her head. It was difficult to speak past the lump in her throat. 'No. No regrets.'

He bent and kissed her lightly. 'Good. But you'd better go below before you lose that towel completely and I take advantage of you.'

Again. But she did not say it. As she stood under the shower she did not know whether the tears that kept starting to her eyes were of joy or of the regret she had denied. If physical pleasure could achieve perfection, then what had happened on the beach should be the summit of all her dreams. But it had solved nothing. All the anger and accusations and misunderstandings were still there, perhaps even reinforced by her total surrender.

She couldn't flee, nor stay in the shower for ever. Eventually she had to return to the main saloon, although she dressed more carefully than usual, pulling on jeans and a shirt rather than the shorts and brief top which were her custom.

He was standing staring out of a porthole. When she came in he turned, but the frown which creased his brow didn't lift for a minute or two. Then he smiled and held out a glass.

'A drink? You probably need it.'

She needed something, if only to give her hands something to do and herself something to look at other than the too understanding expression on his face. It was absurd to be so nervous; even when he had been at his most hostile she had never felt this uncertain. Gratefully, she sipped from the cool glass.

'Thanks.'

'You're welcome.' The continuing unaccustomed gentleness made her eyes sting with foolish tears again. 'I'll cook tonight,' he added abruptly. 'Sit down and make yourself comfortable.'

Hurt and confused, sudden anger helped. 'I'm not an invalid,' she snapped. She *needed* to be busy with something. But he took the step which brought him over to her and held her face in both his palms so that she was forced to meet his eyes. Neither the contempt nor the mockery that she feared were visible, and the tension which had been holding her rigid began to relax.

He kissed her forehead and then, still watching her closely, said, 'No, I know you're not an invalid.' The ghost of a chuckle escaped him before his expression became serious again. 'But it's been a long time for you, hasn't it? Did I hurt you?'

Embarrassed, she flushed, but he wouldn't let her look away. 'No,' she denied. The look in his eyes drew more from her than she had meant to give. 'It's just that since my fiancé, David...' She didn't know how to finish and was both grateful and relieved when he drew her into a warm hug before releasing her and pushing her gently towards a chair.

'So I'm doing the cooking,' he said firmly, as though concluding a conversation, and, oddly comforted, Alix didn't argue.

His concern continued throughout the evening, but to Alix it all passed in an oddly dream-like state. She hardly knew this side of Jake—but how much did she know of him at all? She supposed they must have talked during the meal, but later, as she lay in her bunk, she could hardly remember what they had said. Certainly neither of them had come near to mentioning those timeless minutes of passion on the beach. When he had noticed her evident tiredness and ordered her to bed with brusque kindness she had tensed for a moment, but it didn't seem to have occurred to him that she might expect him to accompany her. Now she wasn't at all sure what any of it had meant, and she was too weary to try to unravel the complicated knot of emotions which she sensed lurking behind her odd detachment. Drifting towards sleep, she found herself wondering idly just how strong the drinks Jake had persuaded her to accept had been.

She felt no worse for them when she woke next day. Jake was moving around on deck and she had clearly slept late. She stretched luxuriously and small, unexpected aches brought back scorching memories of the previous day. In the cabin's dim light she flushed, wondering just how she was going to face him and how much more damage that hopeless, unconditional surrender had done to his feelings for her. Last night he had been kind, but she had learned not to trust his moods. And how did *she* feel about it? That was almost as difficult as Jake to analyse. Not regret, no. Although she had never meant it to happen, the memory was already too precious for her to wish it undone. But the knowledge of just how little she meant to him, beyond the obvious physical attraction, cast a shadow of tawdriness over something in which, for her at least, far more than her body had been involved. Just how much more was something she wasn't yet ready to face.

Impatiently, Alix pushed the sheet aside. It was past time to get up and get busy. If she didn't want trouble—however she defined it—then she certainly didn't want Jake coming down to her cabin to find out if she was all right or order her to work.

There were no orders. In fact Jake hardly said a thing, and that was even more unsettling than any imagined confrontation. Had he really taken all that he wanted from her yesterday afternoon? Was this the 'deal' he had always intended? If he so much as mentions that interview, Alix thought grimly, I'll kill him. She glared around at the idyllic setting which had become a trap and wondered just how much longer they would have to endure it.

Not much, it seemed. Jake had disappeared into the engine-room soon after she had come up on deck, and the occasional burst of life from the machinery suggested that the repairs were well advanced. Alix had never realised how much she would come to welcome the noisy intrusion into the peace of the day.

Later that afternoon he emerged, wiping his hands on an oily rag. Sweat streaked his chest and darkened his hair. Alix's own hands tightened involuntarily on the paintbrush she was holding.

'That's it,' he declared. 'I've had enough.'

'The engine's ready?' she guessed. Hope warred with a sudden sense of imminent loss.

He shrugged. 'I don't know. All I know is that I don't intend doing anything else to it today.' He glanced at her work, which was nearly finished, and said abruptly, 'We both need some time off. Have you ever been skin-diving?'

She shook her head. 'No.' But he was right about their needing the 'time off'—preferably from each other. Right now she'd do anything to break the uneasy tension of the day. Perhaps, like her, he was finding the confines of the boat stifling.

'Well, now's your chance,' he decided. 'It's about time we had a look at the reef in good weather.'

She certainly never wanted to look at it in bad weather again. Jake had disappeared below and she turned to tidy up the paint pots with sudden enthusiasm.

It didn't take long to put towels and masks and flippers into the dinghy, and then Jake rowed them over to the edge of the reef. Twenty yards away the dark blue of the deep water still looked slightly threatening, but here Alix could clearly see the coral which was sometimes only inches below the surface; small fish swam among its fronds, and she was suddenly all eagerness to see it more clearly.

'Hang on a moment.' Jake stopped her as she reached for the mask. 'You can't swim out here with that bracelet on.'

She looked at the plain gold chain on her wrist. It was one of the few pieces of jewellery that had not been sold after her father's death, and she seldom took it off. 'Why not?' she wondered defensively.

'Anything loose or glittering can attract danger,' he told her drily.

'You mean sharks?' Suddenly she wasn't quite so sure how much she wanted to look at the reef.

Jake's lips twisted in amusement at her obvious alarm. 'Not usually. They don't often come inside the reef.' Her

relief wasn't allowed to last long as he went on, 'No—
it's barracuda you need to watch out for. They're very
fast and very mobile and are made up mainly of muscle
and teeth. They don't have particularly engaging tempers,
either.' Nor did he, as a rule, but Alix decided not to
make the comparison aloud, purely in the interests of
harmony. A sudden twitch to his sensuous lips made her
wonder whether he, too, had seen the unspoken parallel.
She unclasped the bracelet and tucked it carefully in the
bottom of the dinghy. He rinsed a mask out and handed
it to her. 'Try this for size,' he suggested.

It fitted awkwardly over her hair, but didn't seem likely
to fall off when she nodded. 'It's fine,' she told him,
but he reached out to check for himself, feeling the
tightness of the strap against her hair and making sure
that the mask fitted snugly around her face. There was
something both remote and intimate about his hands
against the back of her head and along her cheeks. Alix
was glad when he drew back and she could lift the face
plate for a moment and breathe easily. She hoped he
attributed the flush he might have noticed on her face
to nothing more than the unaccustomed equipment.

'Rinse it again before you put it on,' he instructed,
'then it won't mist up. The snorkel's easy to use—you
won't drown.'

Not in the water anyway, she thought, taking the pair
of flippers he offered and realising again just how exactly
his eyes took on the colour of the water around them.
At the moment they were a clear, rather remote aqua-
marine, and it was hard to believe that she had seen them
so recently reflecting the storms of anger and desire.

The flippers felt awkward at first, but as soon as she
began to swim she was amazed at the extra power they
gave her.

'It's fabulous!' she called over to Jake, who was
watching her closely.

'Let's go, then,' he replied and set off towards the reef.

Another new world awaited Alix. Coral, seen previously only from the surface, revealed itself in all its variety of colours and shapes, coiling and looping and spreading in delicate fans and branches. The colours ranged from bone-white through greens and yellows to the less common—but more familiar—deep pink of jewellery. Black sea urchins bristled with threatening spines amid this fantasy forest and anemones waved delicate, seeking tendrils. Among everything darted schools of tiny jewel-hued fish mostly unaware of the two humans drifting above them. Some, however, seemed curious and Alix found herself being peered at through the perspex of her mask by a cluster of brilliant blue and green fish. She couldn't help smiling in response—and found herself with a mouthful of water. She surfaced to clear the snorkel and spit out the salt water.

Beside her, Jake watched with evident amusement. 'You can't laugh and skin-dive. Or talk to the fish,' he added drily.

There didn't seem to be any suitable response to that, so she put her face down again, finning slowly over the reef. Once she put her hand out towards a particularly attractive piece of coral. At once a hand on her wrist stopped her. She turned to look at Jake, her eyes wide. Unbidden memories of him preventing her touching the manchineel bushes—and what had followed—made her tug instinctively to be free.

Perhaps her face betrayed her. He let her go at once and took out his snorkel to explain, his voice as cool and neutral as yesterday it had been passionately angry, 'Coral cuts go septic quickly and all coral is sharp. That pretty stuff you were about to touch also happens to be poisonous.'

'Thanks.' She meant it.

He didn't interrupt her again as she swam over the reef, but she was constantly aware of—and both reassured and disturbed by—his near presence. He was seldom more than a few yards away and she felt, though she could not see, that his eyes lingered on her rather than the delights of the beauty around them.

Eventually, by unspoken mutual consent, they swam gently back to the dinghy. A return to the yacht meant a return to work, so they rowed slowly to the shore. Unfortunately, the fragile ease that had begun to grow between them didn't last. As they lay on the beach, drying off under the late afternoon sun, it was no longer possible to ignore the previous day. At least, it wasn't for Alix. She had no idea at all what Jake was thinking. She stole a glance at him and wondered if he was thinking at all; he looked asleep. His eyes were shut and he was lying on his back with his hands tucked behind his head as though he was wholly unaware of all the tensions and undercurrents that she was beginning to feel tugging at her.

They ought to talk. She shut her own eyes, a wry smile tugging reluctantly at one corner of her mouth. Since when had they been able to talk without arguing? Even yesterday's passion had begun in anger and misunderstanding—and had resolved nothing. No. Just a day or two more; that was all she had to cope with. And if Jake was going to pretend nothing had happened between them, surely she ought to be glad? She stirred uncomfortably, knowing that Jake might be able to ignore what had happened but that there was no way she could forget it.

Beside her, Jake opened his eyes and stretched. 'We'd better go back,' he decided, bending to pick up his towel and walking off towards the dinghy without waiting for her agreement. Well, at least action was easier than lying there trying not to think. Alix walked down to the wet sand edging the beach where he was pushing the dinghy back into the water. When it floated, rocking gently, he turned, holding out his hand as though to help her in.

Abruptly, she was afraid to touch him. Not because of any revulsion, but because of that growing tension. The air between them was charged, and no one deliberately put their hand in contact with a live wire, did they? No one sane did—and Alix felt as though it was suddenly desperately important to cling to the sanity that had guided her all her adult life. Until yesterday.

She dropped her towel into his hand and scrambled awkwardly into the little boat without his help. She saw his hand clench tightly on the soft fabric before he tossed it on to a seat and bent to pick up the oars. As he rowed the short distance back to the yacht, Alix could feel his gaze on her, sensed the frown between his brows, but wouldn't look up or answer it. She fiddled around, brushing wet sand from her toes.

'Sit still, can't you?' She froze at the abrupt command. This time she did look up at him, but he was turned impatiently away, glancing over his shoulder at the yacht as they came alongside.

'Sorry,' she muttered and, when he stepped lightly on board to make the dinghy fast, she retreated quickly from his unspoken questions to her own cabin.

Avoiding Jake was not only cowardly, it was impossible. She knew that. It really wasn't like her to avoid confrontations, but she had lost almost every encounter with him so far and somehow didn't feel up to another one yet. Not until she had worked out just how much she had lost to him on the beach yesterday.

Of course, she couldn't hide for long. There was a meal to prepare, the evening to get through. Somehow she did manage to cook something, but the growing tension didn't dissipate as they sat together and made

awkward conversation. Whatever they said was brittle
and full of silences, as though he, as well as she, was
searching for hidden meanings and betrayals in every
word. Eventually she cleared away the plates, clumsily
dropping a knife to the floor when she had to reach
across him for a moment. In the strained silence, its
clatter was loud.

Jake stood up. 'I'm going for another swim,' he said
abruptly. 'Goodnight.' He was gone almost before she
had straightened from the floor, trying to think of some
crack about avoiding the washing-up.

In fact he'd been scrupulous about sharing the chores
since they'd been stuck here, and she could only be relieved that he'd found a way to break the atmosphere.
Alix scraped the food scraps into the bin, hearing the
faint splash of his dive. At least she needn't worry about
his getting cramp from swimming immediately after a
meal—neither of them had eaten anything worth calling
a meal. She doubted if he even remembered what she'd
served—and he had pushed aside. She shrugged. The
couple of mouthfuls she had tried had tasted like cardboard. And her cooking wasn't *that* bad.

She sat up for a little longer, pretending to read. The
book on her lap lay unopened. Her thoughts were equally
unreadable, even to herself—and she didn't think she
was ready to face what she might discover if she asked
herself what she really wanted to happen next. Not to
mention the pain of knowing she couldn't have it. Jake
thrived in a world she had grown to distrust, a world of
manipulators and victims. Her own father had been one
of the latter and she had seen at first hand how totally
people could be rejected once their usefulness was over.
Her father had not been able to live with it.

Alix shuddered at the memory and stood up, retreating to her own cabin even though she knew, without
analysing how, that Jake wouldn't come back on board

until all the lights were out. She brushed out her long hair, letting it fall almost to her waist, remembering how Jake had run his hands through it and how she had let it drift across his body until he had sworn and held her closely. She shook the heavy, dark fall of it back across her shoulders. It was time she had it cut. That would at least give her a new image back at work. It would certainly be a change and short hair would be so much simpler. Somehow the picture of herself in her neat city suit with a glossy new hairstyle, a notebook in one hand and a phone tucked under one ear wouldn't quite come into focus. She smiled ironically at her own folly—if anything was unreal it was this crazy expedition and its consequences. Beside that, even the Stock Exchange seemed rational.

Turning to get into her narrow bunk, Alix noticed the small shell she had put out on the locker top as an ornament, Jake's gift from that first enchanted morning together. She picked it up, cradling it gently in her palm. They had seen nothing as delicate as this in their excursion to the reef. Perhaps shells like this weren't made to stand up to the violence of storms. Ruefully, she replaced it, getting into bed and switching out the light.

The velvety darkness seemed absolute. A slight breeze drifted in through the open porthole and the only sound came from the occasional ripple of the water below. Not a single rope tapped its message against the mast or creaked as the yacht swung gently.

Alix had no idea how long she lay there, staring into nothing. She didn't even know that she'd been listening for Jake's return until she felt the hull dip slightly as he climbed aboard. She had heard nothing. Now, though, there were a couple of quiet steps on the deck above her. A pause. She had left her own towel out there when they had come back from the beach. Was he using it? Minutes passed, then the hatch slid back with a loud whisper. He was in the saloon now. His steps stopped briefly and then came nearer. She could almost feel the moment's hesitation outside her door, and then the sense of inevitability with which he turned the handle.

His body was a dark, insubstantial silhouette against the deeper darkness, but when he slipped, still cool from the sea, his hair damp and towel-roughened, into the bunk beside her, there was nothing insubstantial about him. He gave her no chance for welcome or protest and she was glad not to have to analyse her response as he turned into her willing arms and took her mouth with a kind of driven urgency.

He made love to her without a word. In the passionate release from the tensions of the day the only sounds were when she called his name aloud in helpless abandon and the thudding of his heart beneath her cheek as she lay against him afterwards while her own pulse returned slowly to normal. His arm tightened around her when she brushed her lips against the warmth of his chest, and then she slipped effortlessly into a dreamless sleep.

CHAPTER SEVEN

ALIX awoke alone. She hadn't felt him leave during the night, but somehow she wasn't surprised to discover Jake gone. Was this to be the pattern of the few days left to them?

Apparently not. He was sitting in the saloon when she eventually emerged, his hands clasped loosely around a cup of coffee into which he was staring as though he could read his future there. He looked up when she approached, but the lines on his face didn't clear at once as he watched her. He looks tired, she realised, and wondered if he had slept at all last night. Wordlessly, he made coffee for her and passed it across. Uncertainly, she sat down opposite him.

'We need to talk,' he said at last, his voice flat, almost drained of emotion. If it hadn't been too fanciful, Alix would have thought that he had chased the problems of their relationship around so much that he was no longer any more certain than she of anything.

'Yes.'

It was almost as though last night's intense passion had left both of them emotionally becalmed. Perhaps this was the only time they could talk without weapons or defences. There was only one problem. Looking up at him with a smile which mocked them both, Alix said mildly, 'Where on earth do we start?'

Almost everything about their relationship was unspoken, she realised, based on preconceptions and false assumptions which had become barriers neither of them had even tried to break down. Jake's wry smile acknowledged the irony of the situation.

'I guess almost anywhere would be new ground,' he admitted. He hesitated and then went on with uncharacteristic hesitation, 'I suppose what I really want to know is more about you. I know you're not what I thought you were.' The casual words were past before Alix had begun to grasp what they might mean. Jake was taking another drink of coffee, almost, she thought absurdly, as though he needed the energy to continue. 'But that doesn't explain a damn thing,' he added in obvious exasperation. He pushed the mug away with impatience. 'I asked you once why you weren't married,' he began, 'and you didn't give me much of a reason——'

'You weren't exactly listening to reason,' she reminded him guardedly. She had to be careful. Jake, she sensed, was asking for a kind of nakedness that they had not shared even in bed together. She wasn't at all certain she was ready for it, nor whether he was going to be willing to respond in kind.

'I guess not,' he admitted disarmingly. 'But even if marriage doesn't interest you—for whatever reasons,' he persisted, 'the absence of boyfriends still doesn't make sense. You're an attractive, passionate woman——'

'And all of those things are handicaps in my job,' she pointed out with sudden bitterness. When she thought he was going to protest she reminded him, 'They didn't give me much credibility with you, did they?'

He winced, acknowledging the hit, but that didn't stop his questions. He should have been a journalist, she thought with half-amused resignation. 'So after the engagement went bust, you went for a career instead? Or was that why it broke up?'

She shook her head, knowing she couldn't yet tell him everything, not all the humiliating details she had never spoken of to anyone. But she could at least be honest within limits. 'No. The job came later,' she told him.

His eyes narrowed as though trying to guess what she was leaving unsaid—the defence mechanisms that had driven her to try to understand the world that had destroyed her father and made David reject her as useless. But he didn't know about any of that, and she wasn't ready to tell him. He looked thoughtfully at her for a long moment and then, when she didn't add anything to her flat statement, seemed to relax, leaning back in his seat, regarding her with an expression she couldn't quite interpret. It seemed to hold both affection and regret. 'So you've spent the past few years earning a place in a man's world—on their terms?' he recognised.

Suddenly she had to swallow hard. So few people realised the extra pressure being female had brought to her work. Even among her female colleagues she had come across more envy than acceptance, and too many men had made assumptions about how she had got her present job. She nodded, unable to speak for a moment as she looked back on the early days and her struggle to avoid what seemed like inevitable stereotyping, trapping her in a world she no longer wanted any part of. 'It would have been easier to end up running the "female interest" stories,' she admitted.

'And you weren't going to use your body to influence your career,' he put in wryly. Startled, Alix glanced sharply up at him, hope mingling with suspicion. The clear blue in Jake's eyes mocked only himself. Then he added, against all expectation, 'I was way out of line there. I'm sorry.'

An apology was the last thing she had ever expected from Jake Hunter. 'Are you?' she wondered cautiously.

His lips twisted as though her scepticism hurt. 'Yes. I don't suppose I've given you any reason to believe it, but I came ashore that afternoon to apologise.' Her disbelief must have been evident. 'I think I began to believe you almost as soon as I cooled off after the first shock of realising just who the woman on the beach really was,' he added slowly.

'You certainly hid it well,' she reminded him.

'Yes, well. Perhaps I needed some sense clouted back into me.' Alix flushed, remembering the blow that had stung her hand and left its mark against his cheek. 'And perhaps I was just trying to resist this.'

'This' was a pattern trailed with one finger down her forearm where it lay on the table. 'This,' as she knew only too well, was also the uncontrollable leap of flame that accompanied it. She couldn't help herself. As the caressing touch reached her wrist she turned her hand palm up, taking his in her firm clasp.

She looked at their hands, linked together on the table. 'Why resist it?' she asked as the long moment stretched out between them, recognising that it was beyond their control.

'I don't know—I'll remember one day.' His smile was gentle as he lifted her hand to his lips for a kiss—the first, she realised, he had given her as an equal.

Yes, they would both remember all the complications and impossibilities sooner or later, but now was all they needed to enjoy what was left of the days together that the storm had given them. Work still had to be done on the boat, but today whenever Alix looked up she seemed to find Jake's eyes resting on her with gentle warmth, and she laughed when she heard him singing as he worked.

'Don't mock, woman,' he ordered. 'You're privileged to hear me.'

'Yes. Only your bathroom's suffered till now,' she retorted. If she enjoyed his off-key rendering of Puccini that just showed how far gone she was—and she certainly wasn't going to let him know that.

Not that he needed encouragement. He insisted that they take the afternoon off and together they explored the tiny islet which sheltered them. Later they lay on the shore, relaxing and talking before returning to the boat.

He was surprisingly easy to talk to. It was as though those few minutes this morning—despite everything that had been left unsaid—had released something in both of them. Although she still could not bring herself to talk about her father's suicide or David's desertion, Alix told him more than she had ever told anyone else of the struggles she had had to gain her present position and her pleasure in her growing success.

'No wonder you reacted when I turned you down,' he realised.

'No wonder at all,' she agreed. 'You're lucky I didn't obey my first instincts and brain you with my tape recorder,' she added drily.

They were lying together on a shaded rock. He trailed a hand across her thigh, watching the expressions chasing each other across her face.

'So why didn't you?' he wondered as her breath caught in her throat.

Concentration had never been more difficult. 'Heaven knows,' she muttered, turning in his arms. She propped herself above him, taking her weight on her hands and looking down into his laughing face. 'Perhaps I fancied you?' she challenged.

His arms tightened, pulling her down on top of him. 'I certainly hope so,' he murmured before his lips found hers in teasing anticipation.

Passion and laughter mingled throughout that afternoon. Alix let Jake into areas of her past that she had hardly realised that she had kept private. In return, she began to glimpse something of his own troubled and confused background.

That evening, tentatively, she asked him again why he was so opposed to the idea of being interviewed by her. She felt the tension in him, the sudden resistance, and wondered whether she had just ruined all that they had built that day. Then, with an effort she could almost feel, he relaxed, although she couldn't help noticing that he sat up to answer her, as though he had to put some distance between them.

'My ex-wife,' he began slowly and with evident distaste, 'interviewed me once for her show. Fortunately, it was a recording and I was able to persuade the company not to put that part of the show out.'

There was a grim set to his lips which told Alix far more than the stark revelation of an episode he clearly wanted to forget. She knew enough about Ellen Carter's show to make a guess at the style of the interview and wondered with revulsion just how much of their marriage she had contemplated broadcasting. She also wondered just how much the incident had cost him—not the financial cost of having the tape destroyed, but the emotional price which he still seemed to be paying. If the fragile relationship that she and Jake shared was to grow at all, Alix was suddenly certain she had to know just what the other woman had done to him to give him such a profound mistrust of women.

'Why did you two split up?' she found herself asking, her voice brittle with nervousness. For a moment she thought he wouldn't answer, but then he shrugged with an assumption of indifference which didn't fool her for a moment. She knew only too well how hard it was to talk about personal disaster—and it wasn't indifference which tightened his expression and turned his eyes glass-clear.

'Ellen married me for my money and my prospects,' he said dismissively.

'It can't have been just those!' Alix couldn't help the incredulous exclamation. Jake would have had to be both blind and stupid—and he was neither—not to know that his attractiveness had nothing at all to do with his bank balance.

Genuine amusement softened his rather bleak expression. He tugged her close again, dropping a quick kiss on her forehead. The smile faded slightly, but he didn't let her go as he went on. 'Perhaps not at first. But it was right at the beginning of my career and I was away more than I was at home and she never did see the need to work that hard—even though she was keen enough to spend the results. And I was naïve enough to believe her when she began to be more "understanding"—until the day when I managed to get home early to surprise her.' His laugh held no humour at all. 'I certainly succeeded. She was in bed with my best friend at the time. He "just happened" to be a TV producer, and she told me that he'd offered her a job.' He turned to Alix with a kind of suppressed hurt and fury, betraying—as she had done—more than he had probably intended. 'She didn't *need* to sleep with the guy to get the job—she had plenty of brains and talent. She could have succeeded on her own in whatever she wanted to do, and she knew she'd have had my support. But she had to go and take the easy way.'

The long silence needed no filling. Alix didn't have to comment and certainly wasn't going to offer excuses for the woman whose vanity and greed had so damaged Jake.

Gradually during the day she had caught glimpses of a childhood of poverty giving birth to a fierce determination to escape from its trap.

'What about your parents?' she wondered.

'I never knew my father,' he told her bluntly. 'My mother wouldn't talk about him. She just told me I had to do better than he had.'

'And you did.' Not knowing must have been the worst sort of torment for a child—he must have seen his father in every down-and-out and criminal he met. Fiercely, she wanted to hug the child he had been; instead she spoke with more control to the adult he had become. 'Is your mother still alive?'

He shook his head. 'No. She died four years ago.' Alix heard the regret which sharpened his voice.

'Long enough to know that you've made it out of the back-streets and into the headlines,' she commented. He nodded, smiling slightly. Then she remembered some of her own problems in researching Jake Hunter. 'Not that the headlines ever gave away much about you,' she added. 'Did you do that deliberately?' As she asked she wondered whether she'd gone too far—for all their growing understanding of each other there were still areas marked 'Private'.

Beside her, she felt him hesitate. 'Off the record?' he asked at last.

It hurt that he even needed to ask, but at least he hadn't slammed the door in her face. She tried to take it lightly. 'You haven't even agreed to give me an interview yet—we were going to "negotiate", remember?' she pointed out. 'The record doesn't even exist.' She had to hope he trusted her enough to believe her. In a way it was true; what was happening here had no relevance to the real world—even if that was where she would have to pay for it.

His quick grin changed the atmosphere. 'You're doing quite well so far.' Then he frowned, as though trying to analyse his own motives. 'I don't really know why I've avoided personal publicity. Perhaps it's because privacy was something I never had as a child—it's a rich man's luxury. Where I came from,' he added with more than a touch of grimness, 'the problem was in *not* hearing what your neighbours were up to.' Alix didn't know what to say. Her own childhood had been protected from every brutality that Jake must have had to learn to deal with. No wonder he had despised her for it. Then his expression lightened. 'If you didn't recognise me on the beach that morning,' he wondered, 'just what sort of person *were* you expecting?'

Every indication that he now really did believe that she had not planned that original meeting gave her more hope. She frowned. It all seemed so long ago now. It was hard to recall when she *hadn't* known Jake Hunter as the infuriating, complex and compelling man lounging beside her. Then she remembered the old newspaper photograph. 'Someone short, balding, paunchy and middle-aged,' she chuckled. 'With glasses.'

His sudden laughter joined hers. 'I'm thirty-four,' he told her. She could judge the rest for herself. Alix allowed her gaze to linger appreciatively for a moment on the broad chest narrowing to a flat stomach and powerful thighs. Tension coiled in her and she had to pause before she could find an appropriately light tone to respond.

'Another illusion shattered.' She managed to sound disappointed, but couldn't quite suppress the twitch of her lips, nor the gasp of pleasure when he turned and pulled her into a sudden affectionate hug.

In its way, the hug was almost more disturbing than the physical passion which flared between them, if only because it seemed somehow more substantial. Desire was one thing; affection implied something else altogether. Alix wondered just what Jake was thinking, and didn't dare ask.

They were on the yacht, enjoying the sunset from the deck rather than the shore for once, with a couple of glasses of Jake's rum punch and a heap of cushions to sprawl on. Alix cuddled closer under Jake's arm as they stared over to where the beach was darkening to a silhouette against the evening turquoise of the sky.

'If someone painted that they'd be accused of romantic exaggeration,' he said quietly. It was the first time she had heard anything like contentment in his voice.

'An impossibly idyllic desert island,' she agreed comfortably, 'with no one around but us.'

He tugged her closer and she felt rather than heard his rueful chuckle. 'That first day, on the beach, I had this fantasy about getting you alone on a desert island,' he recalled.

She groaned, remembering when they had looked back to see only two sets of footprints disturbing the smooth white sand. 'You don't have to tell me. I suspected you were reading my mind at the time.'

His laughter grew. 'So we really were in tune, then?' His shadowed eyes lingered on the shore. 'I didn't exactly intend to shipwreck you, but I can't honestly say I'm sorry,' he said at last.

It was far more than she had hoped for, but she knew better than to make anything of it. 'It's certainly been an experience,' she agreed drily, hearing the echo of his amusement. Then, because she couldn't help it, she had to add, 'How much longer...?' She hated the vulnerability she heard in her own soft question.

Jake turned, brushing a kiss against her forehead before looking back out across the water. Already the night breeze felt cool against her skin. 'I've done as much as I can to the engine,' he admitted, his voice expressionless. 'We could sail tomorrow.' She had guessed it, but hearing it confirmed was different. She couldn't speak beyond the knot in her throat and was glad of the growing darkness which hid the sheen of tears in her eyes from his too perceptive gaze. 'We'll leave in two days,' he told her suddenly, his voice rough as he turned, pulling her down against him among the cushions.

One more day. Neither of them spoke of the future
in those last enchanted hours which ended in a storm of
passion and aching tenderness in her cabin.

He left her to wake alone again on that last morning.
She had had all the endearments and caresses, all the
desire and appreciation that any woman could expect or
hope for, and a lover who had shown her dimensions to
her own sensuality that she had never dreamed of. And
today the idyll would end. Neither of them had spoken
of the future, no promises had been offered or demanded, but Alix was already discovering that that didn't
make things any easier.

Nor did the obvious strain Jake was under. He kissed
her quickly when she came out into the main saloon,
but his movements were abrupt, his voice curt. 'Do you
mind if we skip breakfast? I'd like to get under way
soon.'

It wasn't quite an order but she recognised the tone.
Besides, what was the point of lingering? It was better
to be doing something, even if it meant hastening their
departure from this enchanted lagoon, than waiting
around, listening to everything that was being left unsaid.
Besides, she told herself briskly, trying to recapture her
old, practical self, there wouldn't be much enchantment
left even here when the yacht's own ample water tanks
were emptied. They had several days' supply left, but
even *Shearwater* had her limits.

Positive thinking was all very well, but it didn't stop
her eyes misting after they crossed the narrow channel
in the reef and she watched the little island disappear
surprisingly quickly behind them. One moment, it
seemed, it was a clear shape on the horizon, then a blur,
then a dot which faded rapidly and might have existed
only in her imagination as she strained suddenly unfocused eyes to catch a last glimpse. Beside her, at the
wheel, Jake's eyes were narrowed, focused on the horizon

ahead. He didn't look back at all, not even when Alix
sighed at her last glimpse of the unnamed islet.

The passage back to Antigua was uneventful: several
hours of tranquil sailing over calm seas with a steady
breeze to guide them. Flying fish skipped across the wave
tops in silver showers as the yacht cut effortlessly through
the water. In its way, she supposed, it was the perfect
antidote to the storm, proving just how delightful and
peaceful sailing could be. It was probably irrational of
her to feel this growing discontent and wish for something—anything—to happen so that she had something
to do except sunbathe as far away from Jake as possible
because every conversation seemed strained and arti-
ficial and quickly trailed to a stop. He, she knew, was
finding his own ways to keep busy. There was no real
need for so much chart work and, in these conditions,
the yacht could easily have sailed herself. Alix didn't
know what was irritating her most: his behaviour or her
own.

By the time the familiar entrance to English Harbour
opened up in front of them that afternoon they had
stopped making any pretence of enjoying the sail. It was
a relief to be busy taking down and stowing the sails and
Alix was glad, too, when Jake took *Shearwater* in to
moor alongside the stone quay. She would be able just
to step ashore without worrying about managing the
dinghy. In fact, she realised with a sudden chill that had
nothing at all to do with the weather, her hands stilling
on the rope she was coiling, there was nothing to stop
her from picking up her bag and walking away from the
yacht without a backward glance. She could easily get
a taxi to the airport, and there was bound to be a flight
to London some time.

'All finished?' Jake's crisp voice behind her made her
start. She had not heard him approach. Quickly she fin-

ished dealing with the last coil of rope before stepping back and turning towards him.

'Yes, I think so.' She feared so. She had been fiddling with pointless jobs for minutes now. 'What happens next?' she couldn't help asking.

'I've seen the guys from Customs and told them we've nothing to declare,' he explained. 'If you want to go ashore and phone your paper you might as well do it now.'

Of course. That was the obvious thing to do. She had already been out of touch long enough for Bill Goddard to be panicking—about the story, if not about her. She looked down at her tanned hands, the nails cut short and the skin roughened by recent work. They would be back at work at her word processor soon. Janet, who ran the women's page, would probably take one look at them and tell her where she could get a good manicure. It all seemed a little ridiculous. Suddenly conscious of her own silence and Jake's curiosity, she looked up at him, tossing the heavy plait of her hair over her shoulder with an attempt at casualness which made his eyes narrow.

'Yes. All right. If there's nothing that needs doing on board I'll go and see if I can get through to the office.' She turned to go, then wondered, 'What about you? I should think your people are going to be far more worried than mine about not hearing from you.'

Jake shrugged. 'Another hour or two won't make much difference.' She supposed not, but his lack of urgency surprised her slightly. Not that it mattered. She turned and had stepped carefully down on to a dock which seemed curiously unstable under her feet when he spoke again. 'Alix?' The deep voice held a thread of something that might have been private amusement.

Shielding her eyes against the bright sunlight, she squinted up to where he was leaning against the rails, looking down at her. 'Yes?'

'You might tell that boss of yours that you've managed to persuade me to give you that interview,' he said lightly, and turned away before she could think of an appropriate answer.

Perhaps it was a good thing—she had no idea what to say. Her first reaction was to share his amusement that their relationship now had anything at all to do with either his work or hers; then, almost at once, came the twinge of doubt that would not be quite suppressed. Perhaps, for him, personal and private concerns *could* be kept separate. She knew it wasn't possible for her; for years there had been no conflict because she had had virtually no personal life. Now it was irretrievably entangled with his. Her mouth twisted in a very private grimace. At least the comment meant that he wasn't entirely shutting her out. Not yet. And Bill was going to be delighted.

Bill wasn't going to know anything at all about it for a while. The public telephones at English Harbour were always erratic and frequently busy, but today was worse than usual. Only one was working and the size of the queue for that indicated that it would probably be hours before Alix had a chance of contacting the office.

She hesitated for a moment and then smiled, walking away from the chattering crowd. As Jake had said, another hour or two wouldn't make much difference. Not to Bill. But for her it was a reprieve that might mean another day or two with Jake. She had tried, after all. Not even her conscience could accuse her if she ignored her job for a little longer.

She wanted to see Jake again, to tell him she hadn't been able to make contact, but, perversely, she also wanted some time on her own. For many days now she had not been free simply to walk off and lose herself and her problems either on her own or in a crowd. It was a luxury to be free now to do either. She hesitated for a moment and then turned towards the dockyard gates. Human company could come later; first she was going to enjoy stretching her legs in a solitary walk—especially now that the land had almost stopped its tendency to sway beneath her feet.

For a while Alix wandered aimlessly among the dusty scrub, not really concentrating on anything. Jake was there in her mind, of course—she suspected he always would be—but she didn't want to think too closely about him; the past was too precious and their future parting too inevitable to dwell on. If his plans included her he had given no indication of it, nor did she think she could cope with some transatlantic affair, or being 'available' for however long he was in England. No. What they had had was special; to turn it into something tawdry or furtive would be to diminish it. She, at least, was not willing to do that. She knew what those last days on the island with Jake had meant to her. Not for the first time she realised that she had no idea at all what Jake himself thought. Irritably she kicked at a pebble and swore as her toes, bare in her thin sandals, caught a prickly piece of scrub. She had come out here to enjoy her freedom and not to think about Jake. Why on earth did every thought have to come back to him?

She turned back towards the busy dockyard. If she didn't find some human company she might have to answer that last question herself, and she wasn't prepared for that yet.

She sat for a while with a cold drink at a dockside bar, remembering the past week. It might have been a lifetime. She smiled into the melting ice in her glass, then the pull she had been ignoring for the past hour became too strong and she looked up, dropping some coins on the battered table. Absently, she returned the bartender's wide smile, her thoughts moving quickly ahead of her now, urging her to hurry.

Tethered meekly to the quay, *Shearwater* seemed oddly quiet and empty despite the bustle of the harbour around her. Jake wasn't there. There was a note in his decisive black scrawl on the saloon table, but it didn't tell her much.

Gone to sort out some business. Back soon. Let's eat out tonight. J.

Fine. At least she wouldn't have to cook. Alix was conscious of an odd sense of relief which had nothing to do with her cooking skills and wondered if he too was uncomfortable about their situation now that they were back in the 'real' world. It might be easier if there were other people around them.

Shadows were lengthening outside. She might as well shower and change. Her limited wardrobe didn't allow her much choice, but she brushed her hair till it gleamed, aware that the days in the sun had given it rich chestnut highlights and that her golden tan was enriched by the white of her trousers and the glowing turquoise silk of her shirt.

She was almost ready when she heard Jake come in. He called a greeting, adding, 'Sorry I took so long. I'll grab a quick shower and then we can go.' He had disappeared into his own cabin before Alix emerged. She had never been in there. It was as though, however intimate they had become, he still needed the privacy. She remembered what he had told her of his early life and resisted the temptation to give in to curiosity, or even to offer to help scrub his back.

The images that that idea conjured up brought the colour into her cheeks and sent her up on deck to seek refuge in the dim light of early evening.

Jake joined her twenty minutes later. She was leaning against the rails at the bow of the boat, staring out over the water, and didn't, as usual, hear his approach. Somehow, though, she wasn't startled.

'Getting used to being back in civilisation?' he wondered.

How had he known that she'd been thinking of the island, regretting its peace and the simplicity of their life there? She nodded in the darkness, without much conviction. 'I suppose the ground will stop moving under my feet and I'll get used to the noise eventually,' she admitted.

He chuckled. 'I wonder the same thing myself every year.'

She'd forgotten that he was used to this. What for her had had all the exotic mystery of something rare and unexpected was all part of his annual routine. He might not get stuck on an uninhabited island every year, but she couldn't help wondering just how often he had found romance. He wouldn't, after all, have found it difficult. Suddenly depressed, she straightened and turned her back on the calm water.

'Dinner?' she suggested.

'It's early yet.' He hesitated. 'Why don't you get that notepad and tape recorder of yours and we'll find a private room in the hotel? We could do the interview there. It might give us an appetite.' Alix had the odd conviction that it would have precisely the opposite effect, which was absurd. Why else had she started this whole crazy business?

'Good idea,' she agreed. She hoped she sounded more convincing to Jake than she did to herself.

He seemed to be only half listening, glancing around at the strangely beautiful geometry of the yacht. Then he straightened and moved towards the stern of the boat. 'Great. Let's do it.' She went below to fetch the equipment buried at the back of her small closet. Did he, like her, feel that *Shearwater* was entirely the wrong place for the interview? Was that why he had suggested the hotel?

Interviewing someone who was also your lover was almost impossible, she quickly realised. Fortunately she still had the list of questions and ideas she had prepared two weeks—a lifetime—ago. The discussion was clumsy and stilted, but she didn't think he was deliberately throwing up barriers. In a way she even had the feeling that he was trying to be more open with her than he was used to. As an interview, though, it was a disaster. What he had said, however, could combine with what else she had learned—about his personality, not his private life— to make an article which would satisfy Bill.

The click as she switched off the tape recorder was loud in the strained silence. 'Well, that's over,' she muttered, gathering her things together into a large bag.

'Is it?' Her head jerked up. He was leaning back now, looking relaxed for the first time in an hour.

'I'll send you a copy before we print,' she assured him, uncertain quite what he was asking. 'If you don't like anything——'

'I'm sure it'll be fine.' He sounded dismissive, but he also reached into a pocket and scribbled something quickly on the back of a business card. 'You can send it to this address—it'll be certain to reach me there.'

It was a London address. She looked sharply up at him, but his face was impassive. It was the remote face of the Jake Hunter she had met in the hotel in Guadeloupe, and she was uncomfortable. Then he grinned and was the Jake she knew again.

'Let's eat—we've both earned it,' he decided.

Yes, somehow it had been an exhausting hour. She was glad to leave the oppressive little room that the management had been keen to offer them and return to the familiar, brash noisiness of the restaurant.

Even as they ate, however, some of the awkwardness remained. It was, Alix recognised, as though they were crossing some bridge away from the intimacy they had shared and neither of them knew—at least, she didn't; when had she ever known what Jake was thinking?— what awaited them on the other side.

'There's a flight back to the UK tomorrow.' He spoke suddenly, abruptly, as though it was something he had not meant to say. 'Do you want to take it?'

It was the last thing she had expected, the last thing she had thought of. And yet, in a way, it made sense. Neither of them had ever pretended they could stay here indefinitely. It was just that she hadn't thought that far ahead. Not really. She stared at him blankly; what did Jake want? He was watching her closely, but, as ever, she could read nothing beyond the glint of a challenge in the tilt of his head and the beginning of a question she could not answer in his eyes. *Did* she want to board that flight? The voice in her head screamed an insistent *no*, but she never had the chance to utter it. She was reaching out to take his hand, to take the chance that might brand her a bigger fool than she had been about David, when a heavy hand dropped on her shoulder. She whirled around.

Facing her was a big, burly, red-faced figure with a familiar look of exasperation on his face.

'And where the *hell* have you been, my girl?' he demanded.

'Uncle Bill!' Alix exclaimed and hugged him in astonished delight. She turned back to the table where Jake, who had risen when she had, was watching with polite curiosity. 'It seems that England has come out to get me,' she explained ruefully. 'This is my editor, Bill Goddard.'

The hand that had been reaching out to greet the visitor was withdrawn before Alix could complete the introduction. He looked from the big man to her and back again, his mouth tight and his eyes pale and clear. Around them the noise of the other diners seemed somehow remote.

'You mean,' he said, and Alix heard again the contempt and disillusion that she had thought had gone forever, 'that your boss is your *uncle*?'

CHAPTER EIGHT

BEWILDERED and shaken, Alix shook her head.

'No. He's my godfather.'

If anything, Jake's expression only grew colder. His attention was wholly on her now, as though he had already dismissed the older man from his thoughts.

'Your godfather.' There was a wealth of comprehension in the flat tones. 'And I believed you when you said you hadn't used influence to get your job. You're cleverer than I thought, Alix. You didn't even have to go to bed with the guy.'

He had turned away from the table towards the door before she had even begun to understand what he was saying. And, she thought incoherently, it was lucky for him that he had walked away—otherwise she would have hit him. Again. But she'd be damned if he was going to get away with it.

'Excuse me,' she muttered to her rather bewildered-looking editor and godfather, and headed for the door which was swinging shut behind Jake.

She stood for a moment outside, confused by the sudden darkness. Had he gone back to *Shearwater*? No. She could see the tall figure standing alone by the quayside, hands thrust in pockets, staring down at the water lapping the old stones. For a moment the still tension in his solitary pose seemed to isolate him from everything around him with a poignancy which swamped her anger and distress. Then she remembered his stinging comment in the restaurant. He couldn't just walk away after that.

For once it was he who did not hear her approach. When she stopped beside him and demanded, 'Just what do you think is going on between Bill and myself?' he stepped back sharply as though startled. He hadn't expected her to challenge him, she realised.

It didn't, however, take him more than a second to regain his balance. His voice, when he spoke, was cool. 'Nothing at all. He's family, isn't he—or near enough? You look after each other.'

It was amazing how much feeling could be expressed by such a flat voice. And Alix knew beyond doubt that 'you' were all the privileged, thoughtless people who had ignored his mother's poverty when he was a child and enjoyed their wealth and success in a system which did not willingly offer a place to people like him. And nothing she could say was going to alter his conviction that she was a card-carrying member of that system.

It didn't stop her trying. 'Jake, it's not like that. Yes, he gave me my first job, but, if anything, he's tougher on me than on anyone else on the paper just *because* he's a friend. Can't you understand that?' Impulsively, she reached out a hand, touching the corded muscle of his arm before he again stepped backwards from her. This time the gesture was deliberate, explicit. She let her hand fall helplessly to her side. His were still in his pockets and she suddenly knew they were clenched tight, as though he didn't quite trust his own reactions. Somehow the caged violence was more intimidating than any direct threat. 'Won't you let me explain? she pleaded, hating the note of desperation she heard in her own voice.

His held no more emotion than before. 'What's to explain? And somehow I think I'd rather stick to trusting the evidence of my own eyes. As I should have done all along,' he added brutally.

Clearly all his original doubts and assumptions were back in place. Alix swallowed hard against the sting of tears, anger and despair mingling in a cocktail which threatened to overcome her. Fortunately, anger dominated, rescuing her from a display of weakness which he would despise even more than she did.

'You didn't trust your first impression much once you learned who I was, did you?' she reminded him. 'And you still won't. All you want are your worst fears confirmed. Well, too bad. If you can't trust your own instincts or judgements, then that's *your* problem. It just makes me wonder how you ever got anywhere in business,' she added with a kind of exaltation in her own rage. Where there was no hope, there were no inhibitions, she discovered. 'I'll leave Antigua tomorrow as you were about to suggest when Bill turned up. Tonight I'm sure you'll be glad to hear that I'm going to stay at the hotel. And I don't think we'll need to meet again, do you?' She had turned away, but paused long enough to add, 'If you want to cancel the interview you can always tell Bill—after all, he is my boss,' she enjoyed reminding him.

She had taken only a couple of steps before his voice reached her. 'Alix...'

She stopped but did not turn. No optimism could detect any softening in the way he spoke her name.

'Yes?' Gritted teeth made the word a hiss.

'You can keep the interview. Call it payment for services if you like. After all, that *was* our "deal", wasn't it? Goodbye.'

This time she did turn. Had he still been near enough she would have pushed him into the harbour, and damn the consequences, but his deceptively casual long-legged stride had already taken him beyond her reach. Where he had always been.

By the time she had returned to the hotel all she wanted to do was crawl into bed and let the darkness take over. But there was still Bill to cope with. He had observed

her return and watched her tight-lipped request for a
room without comment. Now all he said was, 'Brandy?'

Alix nodded, not quite trusting herself to speak. She
hated the stuff, but it might burn out the pain that was
searing her. After one sip she pushed the balloon-shaped
glass aside, her hands knotting on the table in front of
her. Almost absently she watched her fingers clench on
each other and thought about what she would like to
say and do to Jake Hunter.

As though her thoughts had triggered his, Bill said
drily, 'Can I take it that that was Jake Hunter?'

She looked up, her eyes wide and dark with unshed
tears of anger and humiliation. 'You can,' she admitted
wryly.

'And are you going to tell me just where and why the
two of you disappeared off the face of the earth, causing
despair and consternation to everyone on the paper?'

Moved by the real concern which ran beneath the
lightly sarcastic words, she reached out to touch one of
his large hands. His other hand engulfed hers in a clasp
which revealed his affection more clearly than he would
ever allow in words.

She swallowed, knowing that Bill's presence in Antigua
was due to his fear that something had gone seriously
wrong. He would never know just how right he was.
Alix returned the comforting squeeze of his hands before
smiling with lop-sided resignation.

'It's been an interesting couple of weeks,' she admitted. If Bill noticed that the account she gave of the
storm and the days on the island was entirely factual and
that there seemed to be some details missing, as well as
a total absence of personal comment on Jake Hunter,
he made no comment.

'I've got the interview now, so I might as well come
back to England with you tomorrow,' she concluded,
adding unnecessarily, 'I'm staying here tonight.' He

looked sharply at her, but she held his gaze with one that defied him to ask for any explanations, and, after a long moment, he nodded.

Releasing her hand, he stood up and stretched. 'You look just about all in,' he commented. 'And if you aren't, you ought to be. Just looking at all those boats out there makes me feel seasick. I'll be glad to get back to civilisation and I expect you will be too. Why don't you get an early night?'

There wasn't anything else to do and she wasn't sure how long the icy wall which seemed to have grown around the hurt inside her would last. She took another swallow of brandy, grimaced, and pushed her chair back. 'I think I will. Goodnight, Uncle Bill—and thanks for coming.' She hugged him and quickly turned away, hurrying up the stairs to her room, because she had suddenly discovered that she couldn't trust her voice any more.

The night that followed was one she would never choose to remember. She could not, although she tried, shower away the memory of Jake's last, cruel words and the fear that he had meant them, nor the growing certainty that she had again made a mistake that could shatter her life—and this time she wasn't at all sure she could put it back together again. After the cool, breezy nights aboard the yacht, the small hotel room seemed stuffy and airless and sleep a distant impossibility. She sat by the open window until early dawn began to turn the sky grey-blue. After that it was merely a matter of waiting until she could reasonably expect both hotel and airport staff to be awake.

It was easy enough to get some coffee from the former. It was when she tried to arrange her plane ticket with the latter that the problems started.

'Are you sure?' she asked incredulously. 'There must be *some* seat availability, surely? Perhaps I could go via

Miami or Barbados?' She was an experienced enough traveller to know that the direct route was seldom the only one.

'I'm sorry, ma'am,' the polite voice at the other end of the telephone assured her. 'There are no seats available to London for two days. It is our major holiday season,' he reminded her with a hint of reproach.

'But yesterday——' Jake had offered her the chance to fly out. But perhaps he, too, had just assumed there would be space.

'I'm sorry, ma'am,' the voice repeated with slightly less patience.

Resisting the urge to swear at his restraint and obvious lack of real concern, Alix managed to say, 'It doesn't matter,' and put the phone down. Her palm was damp from the force with which she had gripped the receiver as though trying to squeeze the response she wanted from the anonymous voice at the airport. 'Damn.' The comment was heartfelt. What on earth was she going to do? She couldn't stay a prisoner here in the hotel and there was no way she could stay on Antigua for two more days and manage to avoid Jake. He wouldn't seek her out, of course, but that wouldn't make their inevitable meeting any more bearable.

'Something wrong, dear?' Bill's reassuring tones interrupted a growing spiral of panic.

'It's just that I wanted to fly out today and there don't seem to be any seats free,' she said with only a hint of unsteadiness in her voice.

He raised an eyebrow sceptically. 'Flight in didn't look that crowded,' he commented. 'Let's see what I can do— you go and get some breakfast or something; I'll see you in a minute or two.'

Food would choke her and she'd already had enough coffee, so Alix settled for a glass of freshly squeezed juice which she took out to the cool shadows of the hotel's sheltered back garden. Bill rejoined her almost as quickly as he'd promised.

'That's settled,' he said in satisfaction, taking the seat opposite hers.

'What is?' Eagerness and doubt mingled in her voice.

'Your ticket, of course.' He signalled to a waiter and ordered a large breakfast while Alix tried to control her impatience.

'But he said——' she began.

Bill gestured dismissively. 'I know. No seats. But there was no problem at all in transferring my ticket to your name, and another couple of days of tropical ease won't worry me at all. Ah, breakfast,' he added as the waiter reappeared with a large tray.

Bill hated the heat and never took a holiday. It was well known on the paper that twenty-four hours away from his desk gave him withdrawal symptoms.

'Thanks,' Alix managed, touched as well as relieved by his generosity.

'No problem—have some toast,' he offered.

She shook her head, leaving him a few minutes later to return to her room. It was more impersonal even than most hotel rooms since it contained nothing of hers. All she had was her notebook, her recorder and her handbag. Fortunately, that contained her passport. She would rather leave everything behind than go down to *Shearwater* and ask Jake if she could collect her belongings. No, she would sit up here until she could decently call for a taxi to take her to the airport.

Her window overlooked the main part of the dockyard. She couldn't see *Shearwater* but she could watch everyone wandering around—some obviously busy, most just drifting around admiring and commenting on the well-preserved buildings. At other times the scene would have fascinated her; now it was something to focus her eyes and the surface of her mind on, a way of avoiding touching the raw places beneath. She needed time and distance before she could think of Jake again.

She got neither. The tall, blond man with the rakish tilt to his jaw striding across the grass towards the hotel was unmistakable. Alix froze. If he was looking for her there was nowhere she could hide. She cursed herself for waiting here, for not going straight to the airport and losing herself in the anonymity of holiday travellers. He had stopped outside the doorway and was talking to someone; she couldn't see who. Cautiously, she leaned nearer the open window. Most of the conversation was a low rumble, but then his companion must have said something which seemed to startle him, because she heard Jake's next words clearly.

'St John's? Are you sure?' Another mumble in reply, then, 'Thanks, I'll do that.' He was striding purposefully towards the dockyard gates before Alix fully realised what she had heard. She had no idea what the conversation had been about, but if he was going into town it meant that she had time to go aboard the yacht and collect all her things. Suddenly she didn't want to leave any trace of herself with him.

She gave him another twenty minutes to change his mind and then, when there was no sign of his return, went cautiously downstairs and out of the hotel.

Shearwater gave her familiar curtsy of welcome as she stepped on board, but there was no other movement on the yacht. Alix hesitated and then stretched out a hand to push back the main hatch.

'Jake?' she called softly, knowing that he was not there to answer, yet half fearing that she had been mistaken after all. Silence and dim shadows greeted her as she stepped out of the bright sunlight and into the main saloon. Her own little cabin was undisturbed and it took only minutes to pack her bag with the few clothes she had brought. She even stripped the bunk, covering it with a brightly patterned spread so that there was no evidence at all that she had ever been there. Except for one thing.

On the small mahogany locker beside the bed was a cardboard box. With hands that shook slightly, she opened it, staring down at the delicate shell inside. Some things had been real, after all.

She must have been too absorbed in her own emotions to notice the boat's movement. She wasn't aware there was anyone else on board until he spoke.

'What are you doing here?' The question was curt. Alix turned round to stare at Jake. There was an expression on his face that she didn't understand. He looked watchful as much as hostile, she thought.

She lifted the little box. 'I came to collect the last of my things,' she said sadly. 'Something to remind me of something that never existed.'

'What do you mean?' He made no attempt to touch her, but she had the feeling that he was alert to any move she might make.

She stared at him. He still had the power to make her heart beat faster, just standing there. It wasn't fair. 'Did everything matter so little to you that you couldn't even try to trust me?' she demanded, her voice passionate and hurting with the words she hadn't meant to say.

'Why should I?' He was suddenly angry. 'Aren't you just off back to the bright lights with your "boss"?' The last word was a sneer.

Her laugh was bitter. 'It's funny how you find that so easy to believe when you've obviously believed nothing else I've ever said to you.'

'I *did* believe you,' he protested, but she was too angry and hurt to let him speak.

'Of course,' she agreed. 'So much that you let me pour out things to you that I've never told another soul, but not quite enough even to offer me a hearing.'

'Last night——' he began.

She didn't want to talk about last night. She turned away, not wanting him to see the pain she couldn't hide.

Rough hands were on her shoulders, urgently turning her back to him. 'Alix...' he began, but the little box had fallen from her fingers at his sudden movement and she was staring at the fragments of shell which littered the cabin floor.

The hands on her shoulders gentled and she looked at him, her eyes bleak. Was this how you felt when someone died? The bold lines of his face held concern and something which she was too tired to interpret. For once the daredevil blue eyes seemed shadowed.

'I loved you, Jake,' she told him, and bent from under his hands to kneel among the fragile pieces which crumbled as she tried to gather them up. 'I loved you,' she repeated, acknowledging it to herself for the first time, her head bowed. Then she looked up, unaware of the tears which coursed down her cheeks. 'But this is all we ever had, isn't it? Something too fragile to survive.'

She heard him swear savagely and then he was bending, lifting her from the floor high in his arms so that she was cradled against him as he carried her across the broken shards to the bunk. His mouth took hers with a kind of primitive passion as he set her down on the cool cotton, his lips demanding—and getting—a flame of response from hers. In that long kiss he seemed to take in all her pain and anger, turning it to need and a desire that was beyond all words.

His lips drank the tears drying on her cheeks before returning to her mouth again, and urgent hands reached for the fastening of her clothes. Her own body leaped in exultation, like the incandescence of a fire before it

consumes itself. The narrow bunk held their sweat-damp
bodies close to each other so that she could feel the
roughness of his chest against her breasts and glory for
that moment in the contrasts between them—his hard
strength against her yielding softness. And then he had
moved over her, his body blocking out the glimmer of
sunlight on water which danced on the ceiling, and the
storm they had passed through at sea seemed to consume
them both. Small cries and the feel of warm skin under
demanding hands, a total loss of identity which became
utter self-revelation, caught Alix in a relentless whirl-
wind in which Jake was the only haven as well as its
vortex. Then the wind died and they were both washed
up on the dry shores of reality.

Of course it solved nothing. Alix knew that even as
she held Jake against her for a few precious seconds
longer. When he lifted his head, he must have read her
thoughts in her face.

'It's not enough, without trust, is it?' he said quietly,
and her own throat ached with the raw suffering in his
voice.

She shook her head. 'No.' Passion was dust and ashes
as well as torment when it was the only thing that drove
them together.

Wordlessly, he stood up, gathering his scattered
clothes, looking down with something approaching
sadness at her naked body. For the first time since they
had become lovers, she felt a flush of embarrassment
under his scrutiny and reflexively pulled at the bed-
spread as though to cover herself. He saw the gesture
and a wry smile of understanding touched his sensuous
mouth.

A last flicker of resentment flared in Alix. He saw too
much. Defiantly, she swung her feet to the floor, standing
naked in the small cabin and forcing him to move to
the doorway.

For a moment she thought he might go no further, but then he turned and went out, leaving her to dress in privacy. He was waiting in the saloon when she emerged.

'Are you all right?' he asked gravely. 'Do you want me to walk you back to the hotel?'

'I'm just fine,' she said in a dreary voice, both of them knowing it was a lie. 'I'd rather be alone.' That at least was the truth.

She walked back to the hotel, checked out, and caught a taxi without feeling a thing. Everything, even the note she left for Bill, was done with a kind of automatic efficiency that demanded no emotions at all. Neither the long wait at the airport nor the boring flight back really registered, and, even when she shut the door of her own apartment behind her, there was only a sort of weary relief. She didn't think of Jake and those last desperate moments because she couldn't bear to. And she didn't cry—because she wasn't sure she would be able to stop. She stayed dry-eyed even when she wrote her article on him with ruthless, detached professionalism, conscious that it was one of the best profiles she had done. She was neither surprised nor pleased when it came back from the address Jake had given her with no alterations and a typed note initialled by someone else: 'OK for publication.'

Bill had arrived back in London two days after Alix and seemed, for him, to be in excellent spirits. He congratulated her on the article, told her she was getting soft from too much time wasted on holidays, and increased her workload so that she had no time to think during the day and was too tired to dwell on the past by the time she got home. No one could blame her if she couldn't control her dreams and she woke too often with a burning sense of loss and the pillow damp beside her.

Jake himself was also back in circulation. Her article had stimulated interest in his actions and now other papers were watching his movements. Alix told herself that she wasn't interested—or, if she was, it was only because of her job—but couldn't disguise from herself the mixture of regret and relief she felt when she learned that he had returned to America rather than England from Antigua.

She had plenty of interested enquiries from colleagues and rivals about what he was 'really like' but managed to fend them off without too much trouble. After all, she thought wryly, she wasn't at all sure she knew the answer to that one herself. Fortunately, it hadn't been hard to persuade Bill to keep quiet about exactly how she had spent her time with Jake, and, beyond some knowing comments about taking the paper's time to get a good suntan, she was spared much comment on her extended absence. Once or twice she caught Bill watching her with a kind of shrewd sympathy, but he said nothing.

After the Caribbean, London was cold and grey. *Life* was cold and grey, but at least it held few surprises and it wasn't going to hurt her. She sat at home one evening, too tired, as usual, to cook a proper meal, and wondered just how long it was going to take this time for the scars to heal. What she had felt for David had been a naïve adolescent's dream; what she felt for Jake was something whose full extent she did not yet dare explore. She looked back on her tranquil life of little more than a month ago with a kind of detached wonder. Life had been so simple before she had been challenged to get an interview with Jake Hunter. Well, she had got the interview—and fallen in love as well. Was it worth it? The pain she refused to face screamed, No! but sometimes memories of those idyllic days on the island almost convinced her that what they had shared had been, if only briefly, too precious to wish undone. At other times she remembered his reference to the interview as 'payment for services' and wondered how she could love someone that cruel. And that was what, since those last moments on the yacht, she no longer even tried to deceive herself about; what she had felt, and unfortunately still felt, for Jake was love. And now all she wanted to know was just how long love could last unfed. Too long, she was beginning to fear.

She had been back in England for three weeks when Bill summoned her to his office. Once she had been excited by such calls—they almost invariably meant some sort of challenge—but now she found herself flinching as she remembered the consequences of the last challenge she had accepted.

CHAPTER NINE

'YOU want me to find out what's been happening at *Turner's*?' Alix repeated. '*Nothing's* happened there for forty years. It must be the stodgiest advertising firm in London. In Europe,' she added after a moment's thought. 'In fact,' she ended reflectively, 'I suppose there might be the beginnings of an article on just how a totally unimaginative firm can survive for so long in that particular business. I seem to remember they even show a profit.' Some firms were definite anomalies, and she did occasionally write articles about unusual or little-known facets of the City. Something on Turner's might just fit into that category.

Bill was shaking his head. 'I'm not sure that's...' he began. Then he stopped. Alix couldn't interpret the way he was looking at her, but he obviously came to some decision, because he nodded sharply, saying, 'Go and have a look and see what they've got there. Someone mentioned them while you were off jaunting in the tropics, and I thought they might be interesting.'

Alix felt her expression tighten at the casual reference to the tropics, but Bill seemed unaware of having said anything tactless. And she was being too sensitive. It was about time she remembered that he neither knew nor cared about the details of what had happened in the West Indies. Not unless it affected her work, of course. From Bill's expression, he was beginning to wonder about that, and she hastily pulled her wandering thoughts together, trying to look interested in the project he suggested while wondering whether he was, after all, just determined to keep her busy. It was usually only the big things—like the Jake Hunter interview, she recalled wryly—with which he concerned himself personally. And no one had ever called Turner's 'big'.

In the end it took no more than a quick search through the paper's files and a five-minute phone call to arrange a meeting. She made a few preliminary notes, thinking that if she'd been feeling more enthusiastic about her work she'd have taken longer to find out more details, but she knew the firm quite well, by reputation at least, and decided to go into it with an open mind. It was a technique that had served her well in the past—sometimes having too many preconceived ideas could stop you picking up on what was actually happening—and she wanted to get on with this. Keeping occupied was one way of not thinking too much about that 'jaunt in the tropics'.

Another night of disturbed and disturbing dreams left her disinclined for anything, except strong coffee, for breakfast. The meeting with James Turner, senior partner and son of the founder, was scheduled for eleven-thirty. For some reason she felt reluctant to go, but decided that was only because she had little enthusiasm for anything at the moment, and at least it was better than sitting at her desk all day. You've got to snap out of it soon, she told herself, grabbing another cup of coffee before picking up her case and heading for the door.

The advertising agency was on the fifth floor of an old but well-appointed office block otherwise inhabited by well-established stockbrokers, accountants and a very old-fashioned merchant bank. As she emerged from the creaking lift, however, Alix was conscious that there seemed to be more life to the place than she had expected. The dark wood and thick red carpet on the floor fitted the image she already had, but there was a gloss about the place that surprised her. Somehow she'd an-

ticipated a film of dust on everything, but there seemed
to be too much bustle here for anything to settle.

The reception desk was formal, highly polished mahogany and gleaming brass name plates, but the girl
behind it was wearing the chicest of business suits, her
hair cropped fashionably short and her eyes alert behind
enormous glasses that Alix suspected held only plain
glass. She greeted Alix with polite recognition.

'Ms Bray? Mr Turner will see you at once.' She led
the way to a panelled door, knocked, and opened it to
usher Alix in. 'Ms Bray,' she announced before leaving
her alone with a smiling, slightly plump older man.

Tension that she hadn't realised she was feeling relaxed, and Alix accepted the chair she was offered, de-
clining the offer of coffee. She'd already had more than
enough—perhaps that accounted for the irrational nervousness she was feeling. Still, she was a little surprised
by her welcome; in her experience journalists weren't
usually treated with this degree of deference. Working
on a paper like hers she usually got attention and, normally, politeness, but she was quite accustomed to
waiting in the reception area for half an hour or more
and to having her interviews interrupted by 'more urgent'
business. Mentally she shrugged. It was an old-fashioned
firm; perhaps part of its appeal lay in preserving at least
the illusion of the manners of a bygone day.

James Turner was charming. He confirmed what she
already knew: that this was a private, family firm
founded by his father and catering to a well-established
clientele. Unadventurous, she amended to herself as she
made a few more notes and wondered whether she could
find anything at all useful to write about here. She supposed she could do something light-hearted, but it
seemed somehow ungracious to mock an organisation
that seemed as courteous as this. Besides, her professional instincts reminded her, there was nothing to

laugh at in a firm which had lasted this long in this market against notoriously short-lived competition.

She looked at the man sitting opposite her. He was smiling gently, but she suddenly saw that he looked weary. He was older than she had first thought, she realised.

As though her expression had betrayed something, he sighed slightly before going on with what he had been telling her. 'Unfortunately, I have no children of my own,' he said, 'so when I retire I shall have to let the firm go public. I hope it works,' he added, with a pre-occupied frown.

The tone of voice told her that he wasn't contemplating some remote future. So there *was* a story here, after all. Giving silent thanks and apologies to Bill's instincts, Alix began to concentrate properly. 'I suppose it's too much to expect to find a private buyer for something of this size?' she probed sympathetically.

He was shaking his head. 'It's not that. It's just that any buyer will certainly want to go public eventually.' A touch of wry humour softened his voice. 'It's what I would probably advise myself if I were twenty-five years younger. But it's not my problem any more,' he added in a stronger voice in which regret and satisfaction were blended equally.

'You mean you *have* found a buyer?' If Turner's was going public, then there was going to be more than a ripple in the waters of the advertising market. A firm like this already had plenty of prestige contacts; it only needed someone with some energy and ideas to turn it into a real competitor. With cautious excitement she wanted to know, 'Is this for publication?'

'Oh, yes, Miss Bray, but I really think you ought to discuss the details with the buyer in question. He said he'd like to meet you.'

The lurking sense of danger crystallised then, followed at once by appalled comprehension. She didn't need the quiet-voiced instruction on the telephone. 'Mary? You can show Mr Hunter in now.' Why, oh, why, hadn't she asked Bill for a transfer to women's fashion, or even the problem page? Except that the paper didn't have any such page and she had far too many problems of her own, the largest of which was just walking into the room as though he owned it. Which, her whirling thoughts reminded her, he did.

It hurt. It hurt more than she had imagined to see him again. She had thought she had learned all about pain during those last hours in Antigua, but one glimpse of that arrogant profile slid like a dagger through all her defences. Automatically, her chin went up and her dark eyes met the blue challenge of his in defiance.

'Hello, Jake,' she managed, pleased that there was no tremor in her voice. 'I didn't expect to see you here.'

Something flickered in his eyes. A salute to her self-control? Amusement at her predicament? The latter, she assumed.

'Hi, Alix. I heard your paper was sending you.'

She had been bound to see him again, she knew. Their worlds overlapped in too many different places. But why did she have to be the one to be unprepared for it? Again. If he thought it gave him some sort of useful advantage, though, then she would have to convince him that he no longer had any power over her.

'Did you? Congratulations on your new acquisition. I hadn't thought all this old-fashioned tradition was quite your style,' she said, reminding him of the scorn he had shown for what he knew of her background.

He glanced round the panelled room. Unbidden, that image of a captain on his quarterdeck, in command of all he surveyed, flickered through her mind. His assessing gaze returned to her, eyes narrowing briefly. 'No?'

he wondered, then shrugged. 'Tastes change, I guess,' he admitted casually.

And what was that supposed to mean? She glanced over to the desk, where Mr Turner had finished collecting his papers and was smiling amiably at them both.

'Well, I've told you all about the firm's history. Mr Hunter—who I see doesn't need an introduction—is the one you need to talk to about the future.'

He was the last person she either needed or wanted to talk to, and the future had always been something they had ignored. 'I think I've enough material for a first article, Mr Turner,' she decided. 'I can always come back if I need more.' A million years from now.

The older man looked towards Jake, who stood in the doorway. His pose was relaxed, the smile looking—to Alix, at least—slightly derisive, but she saw that, like her, James Turner recognised that he was the one in control. He would decide who left the room. Alix had never yet refused a dare, whatever the consequences. When Jake stepped aside to let the older man, who was beginning to look slightly harried, pass she stepped forward to follow him.

She wasn't surprised when a hand dropped to her wrist, holding her back without apparent effort. She didn't even try to tug free—some things were doomed to failure. Instead she glanced down at the big hand spanning her wrist and then up to the cool eyes and amused mouth that were watching her.

'I've seen enough,' she repeated with quiet emphasis and then, with a first show of real feeling, allowed her lips to twist in distaste. 'More than enough.'

The hint of a smile left Jake's face and his eyes narrowed, but he didn't release her. Mr Turner was walking away down the corridor as though to avoid a confrontation he now regretted engineering, but Alix could at least still feel the reassuring weight of the open door against her back. She had no intention of letting it shut herself and Jake alone in the room together.

'We need to talk,' Jake said abruptly.

He had said that once before and the illusion of trust had given them a few idyllic days on the island—but the disillusion had been all the more painful as a result.

'We have nothing to talk about,' she said coolly. She tugged lightly against his clasp and, unexpectedly, he released her, letting her fingers slip unfettered through his. She stood there a moment longer, absently rubbing her wrist, although there had been nothing painful in his firm clasp. No more painful, at least, than standing less than a yard away from him and trying to speak as though he were only a business acquaintance and pretending that her pulse wasn't still throbbing where he had touched her. 'If you want the purchase of the firm covered in detail I'm sure I can arrange for you to speak to someone else on the paper.'

'No.' The tone was flat, indifferent.

'Fine.' She turned and had taken a step away towards the corridor when he stopped her.

'No, it's not. I told you—we have to talk.' The note of command was too familiar and it broke the fragile hold she had on her temper. She wasn't stranded on an island, or pledged to stay on his boat, or seeking an interview any more.

'And I said I didn't want to.' She turned sharply away from him, annoyed that her heart was beating fast, and then suddenly she was reaching out for support as the world spun dizzyingly around her, disintegrating into whirling black spots.

Her thrusting palms felt the wall of Jake's chest, not the expected smoothness of the door, and she flinched away, but his hands were firm on her shoulders, pushing her down into a chair, holding her head low until the room steadied around her. For a long moment after he stepped away from her she stayed still, staring down at the pattern of the carpet through her own hands clasped against her face. Why now? Couldn't she at least have got away from him before pulling a stupid stunt like that? Besides, she never fainted. But the carpet in front of her seemed curiously bleached of colour and the heavy coil of hair against her neck seemed to be weighing her down. She longed to close her eyes, but not while Jake was there. Cautiously, she sat up, aware that her face must still be almost bloodless. She licked dry lips before raising her head. Jake was just waiting there, one hip hitched against the desk, arms folded, a narrow line driven between his brows. Why was he angry with her? Or was he? His voice, when he spoke, didn't *sound* angry.

'Are you all right?' he asked quietly.

She nodded wearily. 'Just fine,' she sighed.

'Sure.' Something in the single, drawled word sharpened her unfocused gaze. Alix took one look at the thin set of his mouth and rapidly revised her estimation of his mood. 'Then would you mind telling me just what the hell you've been doing to yourself?'

Her automatic reaction was defensive. 'Nothing.' She hugged herself protectively and shivered slightly in reaction to the moment's dizziness. 'I told you, I'm fine.'

'I heard you.' Disbelief echoed in the words. 'Stay there a moment.' He walked quickly from the room, the door swinging softly shut behind him.

Now was the time to make her escape, she knew. But somehow she just didn't have the energy. Besides, if he wanted to catch her she didn't think he'd let the thought of shocking a receptionist and a couple of secretaries stop him. Too late, anyway. He was back before she could change her mind. To her surprise he was carrying a glass of water. 'Here, drink this.'

She took the glass and sipped thirstily, feeling stronger. 'Thanks.'

He took in her improved colour. 'Right. Now, where were we?' If only he wouldn't sound so determined.

'*We*,' she managed, sounding more positive than she felt, 'were nowhere.'

A flicker of an eyebrow made her wonder with a moment of near-panic if he was going to remind her of exactly when, and to what extent, they had once been together. To her relief, he let the moment pass. He was still watching her, though, that frown lingering on his face.

'When did you last eat?' he demanded abruptly.

Startled, she looked up. Despite herself, she thought back. She hadn't had breakfast and had been too tired and indifferent to bother with anything but a slice of toast last night. Someone had given her a sandwich yesterday lunchtime. She recalled that with a wry smile; she'd eaten half of it before she'd remembered how much she disliked tuna.

'If it's taking you that long to remember, I'm not surprised you passed out,' she heard him say drily. 'There's a restaurant in the next block; we can get lunch there.'

He was taking over again and she mustn't let that happen. 'I don't want lunch,' she told him. The thought of food, especially in Jake's company, was unsettling.

'I didn't ask you what you wanted. You've got two choices: we stay here and talk, or go out and eat.' The flat tones didn't offer a third alternative.

That didn't stop Alix suggesting one. 'How about if I just go back to work?' she tried, and wasn't surprised when he shook his head.

'No way,' he said simply, and waited.

Carefully, Alix stood up. 'Lunch, then,' she decided wearily. She hadn't really thought she could win, and at least they would be in a restaurant, surrounded by other people, not trapped in a very private office which was

probably sound-proof and where they were certain to be
undisturbed.

'I thought so,' he murmured, a thread of humour
touching his voice as he held the door for her.

He didn't attempt to take her arm or touch her in any
way as they walked back through the office, and even
in the lift he said nothing, just leaning against the wall
of the small compartment, his eyes never leaving her. If
anything, his silence was more disturbing than his
sarcasm.

The restaurant was small and little more than half full.
It was still early, Alix realised, letting Jake pull out a
chair for her at a corner table. At least he wasn't touching
her. He hadn't come close enough even to brush against
her accidentally since those few moments when he had
steadied her against fainting. It was a relief, she told
herself, shutting her eyes briefly against their sudden unexpected stinging.

When she opened them again he was sitting opposite,
watching her, his gaze impersonal, assessing. She
straightened in her chair, feeling at a disadvantage. Her
suit must be badly crumpled and she was sure there were
tendrils escaping from the complex knot of her hair. Deliberately she resisted the temptation to reach up betraying fingers to check it. He was far too quick to pick
up on signals like that. But it wasn't fair; someone who
looked as natural as he did in frayed denim shorts had
no right to look equally good in a dark city suit and
formal tie. And, however unsettled she might have been
feeling, she hadn't missed the appreciative way the receptionist's eyes had lingered on him as they had walked
out of Turner's offices.

His next words revealed that he hadn't been the only
one under observation, although his conclusions were
less flattering. 'Just how much weight have you lost?'
he demanded.

She shrugged. There was no point in pretending she wasn't much thinner; she had seen the new hollows in her cheeks and shoulders when she stepped out of the shower only that morning, and all her clothes were loose on her. 'Thin is fashionable,' she said lightly.

'It doesn't suit you,' he told her bluntly, and she felt the scarlet flush on her cheeks. So she wasn't even desirable any more?

'Thanks,' she said drily and pushed her chair back. She might as well leave now.

'No.' His voice was soft. 'Lunch. Remember?'

She remembered the alternative he had offered and didn't trust him not to use his strength to keep her in the restaurant. She looked around. No one was watching them; the other diners were engrossed with each other and she had no doubt that the waiters were far too discreet to notice the quiet struggle that was going on at their table. Temporarily defeated but determined not to admit it, Alix settled back in her chair.

'Lunch it is, then,' she agreed with what she hoped was a careless smile.

'You need a drink first.' He raised a hand and one of the waiters who had seemed wholly preoccupied elsewhere was suddenly at their side. 'We'll have the menu, but bring a brandy for the lady first.'

The waiter was walking away even as she began to protest. 'I loathe the stuff!'

'Too bad. Look on it as purely medicinal—you've still got about as much colour as a grubby sheet and you look as though the slightest draught would knock you over.'

If she'd wanted any confirmation of her effect on him, she had it. 'You certainly have a way with words,' she commented acidly. 'Any more compliments?'

'Do you want them?' His voice was unexpectedly soft and, looking up, she found her gaze snared in the blue of his and was suddenly breathless. Then the waiter was placing a glass in front of her and offering a hand-written menu, and the disconcerting moment was over. She looked for a moment at the list of dishes and couldn't make sense of it. The words were blurring in front of her. 'Drink your brandy.' Amusement was back in the deep voice. 'Do you mind if I order for you?'

She was surprised he had bothered to ask; at the moment he seemed to be making all the decisions. 'Go ahead,' she agreed indifferently and took a reluctant sip of her drink. Unwillingly, she remembered Bill ordering brandy for her in Antigua. Why did men assume it was the cure for all ills? she wondered idly as she felt the fiery warmth of the alcohol catch at the back of her throat.

It was infuriating to realise, when a bowl of soup was put in front of her, that she *did* feel better. She even felt hungry. She picked up her spoon, looking cautiously at Jake, who hadn't spoken since ordering the meal.

'Go on,' he told her. 'It won't bite back.'

Unlike him. Still, he seemed at least to be sticking to the terms of his alternatives: talk or lunch. And lunch was proving unexpectedly appealing. The bowl of soup was emptied before she knew it and the light omelette which followed disappeared almost as fast. She had just eaten, and enjoyed, a bigger meal than any she had had in all the weeks she had been back in England, she realised. She smiled wryly to herself; it was hardly surprising that she'd lost weight.

Then she caught Jake's glance, which was also lingering on her empty plate with something she interpreted as amusement. 'Satisfied?' she snapped, annoyed that he had been able to manipulate her so easily.

His lips twisted as though he was digesting something far less palatable than the excellent meal they had shared.

'No,' he said slowly, 'but I think we'd better settle that tomorrow. You've had enough for today.'

His tone might be unthreatening, even reasonable, but the faint feeling of contentment that the meal had induced fled at once. 'I'm not seeing you tomorrow,' she blurted, the words tumbling out.

If he heard the hint of panic, he ignored it. 'You are, you know.' His voice was relaxed, but there was something implacable in it that had every alarm bell ringing in her head. 'If I didn't have an afternoon full of appointments—and if you didn't still look as though you'd shatter at a loud noise—we wouldn't be waiting till then. Besides, you need to know my plans for UK investment, don't you?'

Six weeks ago an offer like that would have seemed like the scoop of the year for the paper, and herself. Now she never wanted to hear anything at all about Jake Hunter's plans. They certainly didn't include her, and the only way she was going to recover from this stupid infatuation was to know as little as possible about him for as long as possible. Preferably forever.

'I've got a very promising junior who'll jump at the chance,' she told him, her mouth suddenly dry. He had to know she wanted nothing more to do with him. She'd been too badly scorched. 'I'll send him over.'

'And I'll send him straight back. And give the story to another paper.' He paused, then added, 'I'll tell your editor for you that you turned down the story, if you like. After all, surely your *godfather* won't blame you?' he finished mockingly, leaning back in his chair and regarding her with bland assurance.

He had her cornered and he knew it. It wasn't the sort of story any journalist in her position could afford to turn down and nor was she going to trade on Uncle Bill's affection to get her out of it—even if she could convince herself that his feeling for her would overcome his newspaperman's instincts to that extent. Her career was all she had left and she wasn't going to make the sort of mess of that that she had made of her personal life, even if it meant that she had to interview the man with whom she had made that mess.

'What time tomorrow?' she asked dully.

'Two-thirty. You can come to the head office. I'll show you round.'

Somehow that offer didn't have much appeal either. Alix tried to look professionally interested and avoided the too knowing expression which she was certain she would see if she looked at his face. She reached instead for her diary to make a note of an appointment she knew she wasn't going to forget—no matter how hard she tried. Besides, she wouldn't put it past Jake to come and fetch her if she failed to turn up. She had no idea why he was doing this, but he was clearly determined and, if she had learned nothing else about him, she knew that his determination could more than match hers. Briefly her fingers tightened on her pen as an unwelcome idea crossed her mind. Was this a further instalment of 'payment for services'? If it was, if he even hinted at any such thing, then *nothing*—not Uncle Bill, not the scoop of the century, not the whole of her professional future—was going to make her listen to anything he might have to say.

With hands that shook slightly, she put away her diary and closed her bag. 'Your head office is in the Preston Building, isn't it?' she asked, knowing the answer but determined to show him that she knew her business.

'Yes. The top floor.' She remembered when the new and luxurious block had opened and the speculation there had been about which firms would want, or could afford, the prestigious upper floors.

'I'll be there.' If she sounded like someone promising to turn up for a date at the scaffold, that was his problem.

She picked up her bag and briefcase and stood up. 'Now, if you'll excuse me . . .'

He was on his feet, too, one hand lightly under her elbow, the touch solicitous, impersonal. To anyone watching it must have seemed like the polite conclusion to a business lunch. Until Jake added, 'I'll see you home.'

Startled, Alix stopped short, feeling the colour flooding up into her face. 'No, you won't. Besides, I'm not going home.'

The hand tightened on her arm. Still smiling politely down at her, Jake began to walk towards the door, and Alix had no choice but to follow. 'Oh, yes, you are. I'll phone Bill Goddard and let him know you aren't well.'

'I can do that myself,' she snapped. She certainly didn't much want to go back to work and knew she would accomplish nothing useful even if she did return to her desk, but she had no intention of letting anyone else make her excuses. She closed her eyes briefly at the thought of what the all too efficient office gossip machine would make of Jake Hunter phoning on her behalf.

'Then you'll let me take you home,' he insisted. It wasn't a question. More like blackmail, she thought sourly. It was something he seemed to be good at today, and, as he opened the taxi door for her and slipped in beside her, she realised that, just for an hour or two, she hadn't had any energy left to argue. The taxi didn't move, and she looked up uncertainly.

'I don't have your address,' he reminded her drily.

Embarrassed, she gave quick instructions to the driver and hoped Jake wasn't paying close attention. Not that it mattered—if he'd wanted her address it wouldn't have been impossible for someone like him to discover, even if it was unlisted, and, anyway, today had made it abundantly clear that, whatever his interest in her, it was no longer personal.

He didn't even get out of the cab when it pulled up in front of the town house in which she had a flat. He just said, 'See you tomorrow. If I were you, I'd go straight to bed. Sleep well—and don't forget to eat something,' he added as she opened the car door. The taxi waited while she fumbled with her keys and let herself in, but it had gone by the time she reached her first-floor flat and stared down through the front window on to the empty street.

Alix leaned her head against the cool glass and wondered why she had thought things could get no worse. It had been bad enough loving Jake and knowing that all he felt was something between contempt and desire. Today he had treated her almost with indifference. If she hadn't had that silly fainting fit he probably wouldn't even have felt forced to give her lunch and look after her like a child who couldn't care for herself. He'd certainly made her lack of physical appeal clear enough.

She stared at her reflection in the bathroom mirror and her lips tightened. She could see Jake's point. Her tan had gone and her face was colourless; even her lips seemed pale, and violet shadows made her eyes look huge and haunted. The severe hairstyle, drawn back from her face, mercilessly revealed the features sharpened by weight loss. She turned away with a grimace, unaware of the porcelain transparency of her complexion and the fragile delicacy of her revealed bone-structure. Clumsy with sudden tiredness, she unpinned the rich chestnut coils of her hair, letting them tumble carelessly down her back in vibrant abandon. She would phone Bill and then she would, for once, take Jake's advice. She needed the sleep.

CHAPTER TEN

ALIX awoke next morning feeling surprisingly alert. She dressed quickly, for once plaiting her hair back loosely in the style she normally only used during her time off, and went into the office, parrying questions from Bill without a qualm. She even had lunch with a friend without that sense of indifference and loss which had been her companion for so long. Aware of a faint sense of exhilaration as she stood in front of the gleaming modern building which housed Hunter Enterprises, she would have laughed at herself if she hadn't been enjoying the sense of being really alive for the first time in nearly a month.

Which was all nonsense, of course. Jake had no time for her, despised her, and no longer even found her attractive. She ought to be in despair. With a private smile she pushed through the glass doors and headed for the lift which would take her straight to the building's top floors. The irrational truth was that the idea of exchanging barbed comments with Jake, however painful and predictable the outcome, made her feel more alive than anything else had done since she had last stepped ashore from *Shearwater*.

The lift doors hissed quietly open after the silent ride and she stepped confidently out into the elegant and modern reception area. After all, she no longer had anything to lose.

The secretary at Reception was an attractive replica of the one she had met at Turner's yesterday. Alix was both amused and intrigued by the girl's instant reaction when she announced herself.

'Ms Bray? Of course. I'll take you along to Mr Hunter's secretary at once.'

Personal escort service, no less. Plus what was evidently a healthy dose of curiosity. She wasn't sure how much anyone knew about what had happened in the West Indies—not much, she suspected—but her own research had told her how rare it was for Jake to grant interviews about his plans. Besides, it wasn't unlikely that her own profile of him had already been digested and discussed by most of his staff.

She was both surprised and reassured to discover that Jake's secretary wasn't yet another from the dolly-bird mould. She was smartly and expensively dressed, but also matronly and at least ten years older than her employer. She stood up and held out her hand, smiling with friendly warmth as soon as she saw Alix.

'Ms Bray? I'm so pleased to meet you.' The soft transatlantic voice held genuine warmth. 'I'm afraid Mr Hunter has been caught by an urgent phone call. But I don't think he'll allow it to hold him for long.' The smile seemed almost conspiratorial. Just *what* rumours were going round? Alix wondered, torn between amusement and exasperation.

'Would you like some tea or coffee?' the other woman offered, but Alix shook her head.

Nerves and uncertainty made the idea of anything like that impossible. She allowed herself a private smile, though, at the memory of having had lunch; she had no intention of making a fool of herself, or of handing Jake a ready-made advantage, again. From behind the closed office door she heard the sound of a familiar voice raised in irritation. Alix grimaced sympathetically. She was glad she wasn't on the receiving end this time.

The older woman, who introduced herself as Marian Stokes, confirmed that she had been with Jake for several years. 'It's been interesting,' she admitted, but was clearly not going to be drawn into any more personal comment. She chatted in a friendly way while efficiently keeping her eyes on her computer screen's complex display, and, as she had predicted, it wasn't many minutes before the office door was wrenched open.

'Marian?' the familiar voice, heavy with annoyance, demanded. 'I don't want to speak with Pete Smith again until he's come up with some sensible ideas. OK?'

'OK, Jake. Ms Bray's here,' she added unnecesarily, because Jake had already seen Alix and was opening the door wide to admit her. A moment's comprehensive glance which seemed to take in everything about her gave way to a grin which set her pulses racing.

'Come on in, Alix. And Marian?'

'Yes, Jake?'

'No calls. No interruptions. I don't even want to know if the building burns down or someone assassinates the President. Got it?'

'Got it. By the way——'

'Yes?' A hint of impatience now, and Alix hesitated on the threshold of his office, enjoying the relationship between the other two.

'I can see why you ran up that airport bill.'

'What did that mean?' Alix couldn't help wondering as he shut the door sharply behind him, his own abrupt laugh cut off as he faced her.

'Nothing.' It was curt—something he clearly had no intention of discussing—but not hostile. And, after all, the details of his business were confidential.

'Sorry.'

'Don't be. How are you feeling?' The searching glance again registered her recent weight loss.

For all her buoyant spirits, Alix was suddenly self-conscious. She turned away, looking around the office to hide her reaction. Anything rather than meet his gaze again. 'I'm fine now. And yes, I've had something to eat,' she added quickly before he could ask. This meeting was professional, not personal, she reminded herself. 'I like your office.'

'So do I. But at the moment I couldn't give a damn about it.'

Alix suddenly began to doubt all her confident assumptions about this interview. Guardedly, she asked, 'What did you want to tell me about your business?'

He shrugged, the powerful shoulders moving easily under the tailored jacket. 'Anything you like. Later. Right now I want that talk you've been avoiding.'

Alix discovered she was fiddling with the heavy fabric of the curtains. Painstakingly, her heart thumping erratically, she straightened the crumpled material. Her mouth was dry and she was no longer at all certain that she was going to be able to cope with whatever Jake wanted to say.

'I'd still rather avoid it.' Her voice was clear, careful, and she kept her back to him. Tense and alert, she listened for whatever move he might make next.

As always, she heard nothing. Hands held her shoulders, turning her so that she had to face him. 'Too bad.' Oddly enough the familiar impatient tone was reassuring, enabling her to straighten up and meet his eyes with defiance in her own. His hands had gentled, but he was staring down at her as though he wanted to read her soul. She hoped he couldn't even read her thoughts.

He must have reached a decision then because, before she could ask about the 'talk' he wanted, he asked abruptly, 'Are you pregnant?'

That stupid fainting fit. Now she understood yesterday's impersonal concern. Alix wrenched herself free and stepped back from him. 'Would it matter to you if I were?' she challenged. He'd probably get his lawyer to sort it out—or was this meeting his idea of being noble and doing his duty?

He had made no move to close the gap she had put between them, but he was watching her closely as though trying to gauge her reaction as he answered mildly, 'No, not a damn.'

She believed him and it hurt. She must have betrayed her feelings somehow, perhaps in her stillness, because he gave an exasperated sigh.

'Come here.' She didn't move. He was between her and the door and even if she got through it she didn't trust Marian Stokes to let her pass. But that didn't mean she had to do what he said. Particularly not when it sounded dangerous. 'Let me explain.'

'There's no need.' It was all too clear and she didn't think she could bear to hear whatever it was he thought he could explain.

'Yes, there is. I'll put it as simply as possible—just in case we get caught up in some other crazy misunderstanding. Besides,' he added with an uneven smile which softened her defences before she could steel herself, 'I don't want to spend *all* afternoon talking.'

If he thought he could just take up where they had left things on the island, forgetting all that had happened since, he could think again. He could say what he wanted to now, and then she would have considerable pleasure in giving him *her* opinion before she walked out. His next words, however, left her speechless. 'What I want is *you*. Plus or minus a baby. I suppose I thought,' he admitted ruefully, 'that I might have a little extra leverage if you are pregnant—unless it makes you even more cock-eyed than usual so that you start thinking I'm only being honourable.'

Her heart was beating so fast that she was breathless. Bubbles of incredulous delight were forming in her bloodstream and all she could do was stare at him. He meant it. He was looking at her with one eyebrow raised, as though daring her to take him seriously. She tossed the long plait back over her shoulder, her own smile beginning to break through.

'You? Honourable?' she managed to mock, knowing that her face must be betraying her.

'I said it was cock-eyed. Come here,' he repeated.

Alix stood her ground for a moment longer, facing his challenge, aware of a sudden, giddy surge of power. Then she saw what he had hidden from her: the uncertainty behind the devilry in his pirate's eyes, as if, despite all his assurance, he wasn't absolutely certain what she'd do.

It was all she needed. She took the two steps necessary to bring herself into his arms, which closed around her as though he would never let her go. His mouth was hard on hers, demanding the response she had never been able to withhold. The world spun dizzyingly and Jake was the only stable thing left to cling to. The spiral of need was beginning to tighten its coils in her when he lifted his head.

'Jake...' she murmured in protest, tightening her hands on his shoulders, loving the texture of his hair against her fingers, the hard reality of muscle beneath the fine wool of his jacket.

He bent again, stealing quick kisses from her swollen mouth but preventing her from drawing him deeper, so that she moaned in frustration. Finally, he rested his forehead against hers, his eyes so close to hers that they were a blur of blue and she could have counted every long, fair eyelash if she had been able to concentrate on anything except the rising heat in her body.

'No.' The word was decisive enough, the tone as shaken as Alix felt. 'This time, let's get it right; we'll talk first.'

Reluctantly she straightened, needing the support of his arms as he held her for a moment. Briefly she thought of the contrast with yesterday; there was nothing impersonal in his touch now. But he was right. They had to discover just how much they had beyond the passion which flared at the slightest touch or look. She took a deep breath. 'OK, you win. We'll talk.'

His grin was uneven and the hand he ran through his fair hair wasn't quite steady, but his chuckle was infectious. 'I think that's the first time you've ever agreed to anything without an argument.'

'You were very persuasive,' she managed, hearing the tremor in her own voice. She looked around at the office furniture, suddenly reawakened to an awareness of their surroundings. 'Or perhaps it's just the sense of power that goes with the executive office,' she teased.

He grabbed her hand. 'In that case, let's go next door.'

She hadn't really noticed the door behind his desk. It led, she discovered without much surprise, to a spacious modern apartment. She looked around, admiring the luxurious fittings but unable to see much of Jake's personality in them.

'It's a company apartment,' he told her as he loosened his tie and undid the top button of his shirt. The old Jake of the Caribbean wasn't far from the surface, Alix recognised, hardly listening as he added, 'I'll have to get a place of my own soon.' Then he reminded her, 'You never answered my question.' And his tone was determined that she should.

Still overwhelmed by what seemed, against all the odds, to be happening, Alix was bewildered for a moment. 'What? Oh,' she remembered, smiling gently. 'No. No baby,' she admitted sadly. She had half hoped that it might have happened. Then his arms were gently round her, holding her close in a long embrace which seemed to accept and understand her confusion of feelings. When she looked up at him she even thought she saw a hint of regret in his eyes—which surely had to be absurd. Almost reluctantly, he let her go.

'Sit down,' he said quietly, indicating the wide sofa.

She sat there, just waiting. She still wasn't sure of him, but hope had never beaten more strongly. 'Well?' she wondered as he stood looking down at her, an expression she'd never seen before on his face. Then, in a gesture that was achingly familiar, he brushed back the lock of hair that had fallen across his forehead, a questioning smile just breaking on his lips. He hesitated a moment longer then took the seat beside her, not quite touching her.

There was a moment of silence. He was staring down at his hands, which were loosely clasped in front of him. Then he said, 'You got to me right from the first,' almost as though he was explaining something to himself. 'That's why I reacted so strongly when I realised who you were. I felt as though I'd been set up like a perfect sucker. Again. Deceived by apparent innocence and beauty only to find it hiding scheming ambition. I couldn't even admit to myself just how hard I'd fallen. So, naturally, I took it out on you,' he added in a more familiar voice.

'Naturally,' Alix agreed, not yet quite ready to believe that this might, after all, turn out to be real. 'And there was Ellen, too,' she risked adding quietly when he paused, clearly trying to organise his ideas.

His mouth twisted as though tasting something sour. 'Yes. It's funny; you think you're over a thing like that and it takes meeting someone like you to find out that you haven't really faced it at all. Not that I realised that at once,' he admitted.

Alix recognised, painfully, how true that was; she had
hidden her hurt from David's rejection beneath her job;
she hadn't faced it either. Not until every encounter with
Jake had reminded her of her vulnerability, stirring long-
buried memories. Impulsively, she reached out to take
his hand, which closed convulsively on hers. 'I don't see
why you ever let me near *Shearwater*,' she said, understanding with sudden clarity exactly why he would have
wanted to drive her away.

He turned their clasped hands, looking down at them
before looking up again, his eyes alight with self-
mockery. 'I told you, I fell hard. But I did try to put
you off.'

She remembered his cold hostility only too well. 'You
certainly did—you couldn't know it was the one way
guaranteed to make me stick like glue. I didn't know
whether I was more terrified of you or the boat,' she
admitted.

'You hid it well—but then you always did have guts.'
Oddly it was a compliment that somehow mattered more
than any comment on her looks could have done.

'I still don't see why you let me come with you,' Alix
persisted.

His smile was wry. 'I'm not sure I know. I half hoped
I'd put you off when you turned up on that quay in
Guadeloupe. But somehow...' He didn't finish.

'But...?' It didn't make sense. 'You *despised* me,' she
reminded him in protest.

He winced, but didn't deny it. 'I guess I was con-
spiring against myself. I told myself I wanted to see you
make a fool of yourself, to confirm my doubts, but
underneath I just didn't want you to get away. I think
I somehow wanted to prove you were like my ex-wife
and not the girl I'd met on the beach that morning.'
With his free hand he reached up and traced the line of
her cheek and jaw, just as he had done that morning in

Guadeloupe. This time it was so easy to give in to the impulse to turn her head, pressing a kiss into his palm. She heard his quickly indrawn breath, and his hand lingered warmly against her cheek a moment longer before dropping away. 'Fortunately——' his voice was dry, but his eyes were warm with the familiar flare of desire as well as a tenderness that was wholly new '—you kept proving me wrong. I suppose,' he added with a glint that was all pirate, 'I also hoped that a week in close company might lead to interesting developments. Which,' he laughed, 'it did.'

With feigned indignation, trying unsuccessfully to suppress her own chuckles, Alix attempted—and failed—to tug free. 'You, Jake Hunter, are the most ruthless, domineering, overbearing, manipulative——'

'Quite.' He stopped her with a hard, swift kiss which left her wordless. 'You have a problem with that?' he challenged.

'Do I have a choice?'

'None at all.'

Had she ever? She was mad, of course. *No one* in their right mind could want to put up with someone like Jake. And she wanted to spend the rest of her life doing so? Mad, she decided contentedly. Then she remembered those last days in Antigua and a shadow crossed her delight.

'What is it?' He was as quick as ever to sense her changing mood.

'Trust,' she said simply. 'I can't stay without it.'

His understanding was immediate and complete, and this time he did draw her close so that she was leaning into the warmth of his body. 'I wish you'd told me about your father,' he said quietly.

Startled, she turned quickly in the circle of his arm to stare at him. 'Who on earth told you?' she demanded, and knew the answer before he spoke. There was only one possibility.

'Bill Goddard told me while he was waiting for a flight home,' he confirmed, an undercurrent to his voice that she couldn't quite place.

She thought about the meeting between the two men and couldn't conceal a smile. 'That must have been an interesting encounter,' she commented as neutrally as she could.

She felt his chuckle. 'It had its moments. Still, when he'd finished shouting at me and told me about your father's bankruptcy and death——' Alix flinched and he dropped a soft kiss on her hair, pulling her into the comfort of his embrace '—and about your lousy fiancé, several things became a lot clearer. He also set me straight about your job,' he added, and a note in his voice suggested that Uncle Bill had not minced his words.

'So now you know I'm not a liar,' she commented. She couldn't quite keep the thread of regret from her voice. Confirmation of the facts wasn't the same thing as trust.

His hand cupped her chin, forcing her to look at him. 'I know what you're thinking. That's why I said we had to talk—if only we'd both been wholly honest, and not so scared of history repeating itself, we wouldn't have got into such a mess. But in the end I *did* believe you. I even came round to apologise and see whether we couldn't work it out.'

'When?' The last time she had seen Jake in Antigua had been when she'd left the yacht after the terrible storm of passion which had revealed just how wide the gulf between them stretched. Her eyes blurred at the memory.

He released her chin, holding her head close against his chest. She could hear the beat of his heart beneath her cheek, a steady, reassuring pulse that promised eventual order out of the chaos of their lives. When he spoke, she realised with surprise that he was smiling.

'I guess I do have to explain that remark of Marian's after all.'

Alix straightened, turning to look at him. He actually sounded *embarrassed*. 'Why?' What did he mean? 'Something about air fares, wasn't it?'

He nodded. 'That's it. You remember you told me you were flying out?'

'Yes.' She remembered that confrontation on the quayside the night they had returned to English Harbour all too well.

'Well, next day, after you'd left the boat——' his voice roughened and she couldn't speak past the knot in her own throat '—I came to what was left of my senses and accepted that you *weren't* the same sort of person as Ellen. That you were right: it was my instincts I was refusing to trust, and if they were really wrong, then everything else in my life was probably about to fall apart, too. I decided that we both needed time to calm down a bit, but that I'd see you next day so that we could talk.'

'But you knew I was leaving that afternoon!' Alix protested. He wasn't making sense, and he was still looking uncomfortable.

'No, I didn't,' he corrected her. 'I'd no idea you'd swapped tickets with Bill Goddard—and I thought I'd made sure there were no flights available.'

It took a moment to sink in. Then Alix couldn't help her laughter. 'Are you telling me that you bought up every other available ticket on heaven knows how many flights out for two days?' she gasped. It was a wonderful, unbelievable, extravagant gesture. She hugged him in delight.

'My accountant knows exactly how many flights,' he grimaced, 'and both he and my secretary think I've finally gone mad.'

'Marian doesn't,' Alix reminded him. In fact the woman had sounded positively encouraging, she recalled.

He grinned. 'Not now she's met you. Anyway, like most grand gestures—it didn't work. You went home and I was left with your godfather. He was lucky I didn't beat the daylights out of him when I found out what he'd done,' Jake added, humour not quite hiding the memory of pain and frustration. 'I think he was inclined to do the same to me,' he added ruefully.

'So you lost your temper, he lost his—and you both ended up discussing me?' She could just imagine the scene. How much rum had disappeared during that 'discussion'? she wondered.

'Something like that,' Jake agreed. 'But do you understand what I'm saying about trust?'

Slowly, she nodded. If he had done that just to keep her on Antigua—and he must have done it that first night, within hours of that destructive confrontation on the quayside—so that they could talk, trust must have been there, beneath the surface, even though they were both too cautious of commitment to admit trust easily. She too, she realised, had not given him much trust; she had never brought up the subject of the future herself, never even hinted that she hoped for one with him or thought that he could be relied on to offer anything but a physical relationship. She hadn't even trusted him with as much information about her background as he had given her. She shook her head in regret for her own inhibitions and uncertainties, then, anxious lest he misinterpret her silence, she turned urgently to him.

'Oh, yes, I understand. In fact I wish Bill hadn't been quite so helpful about the plane ticket.'

He chuckled. 'You can't wish it more than I did. Still,' he added, 'he's made up for it since.'

There was a note in his voice which Alix *definitely* didn't trust. 'What do you mean?' she asked suspiciously.

'Who do you think suggested the article on Turner's?' he asked, as though it should have been obvious.

Of course it was. Now. 'You mean that you and he...?' Torn between indignation at being so easily manoeuvred and delight that Jake had made the effort, she couldn't finish. Then she thought of her godfather's collusion in the scheme. 'Bill Goddard,' she decided quietly, 'is a conniving, pandering, soft-centred——'

'Friend?' Jake interrupted.

'Yes,' she had to agree, remembering all that he had done for her over the years. And now this. She was glad that he and Jake had resolved their differences. Then she frowned. Jake might enjoy scheming like some machiavellian plotter, but she knew as well as anyone just how direct his methods could also be. 'You knew where I worked. Why didn't you just call me if you wanted to talk?' she wondered.

'I wanted a good deal more than talk,' he told her drily, the implied promise warm in his voice. 'Besides,' he added, 'would you have agreed?'

She thought of the mood she had been in when she left Antigua, the desolation since then and the attempts she had been making to rebuild the walls that had been demolished during those days on the island. 'Probably not,' she agreed mildly. She would have said no—and regretted it for the rest of her life. There were times, she recognised with wry self-knowledge, when it might not be a bad thing to be manoeuvred by someone like Jake. Although she wasn't going to admit it. Seeing the laughter lurking in his eyes, she guessed that she probably didn't need to.

'And now,' he went on, the laughter fading and something else, familiar and exciting, taking its place, 'I think we've done enough talking for the moment. Don't you?'

When he looked at her like that and his hands moved against her, what on earth was she expected to say? Manipulator, she thought in the few seconds before coherent thought became impossible.

He stood up, lifting her easily with him, and the vision of him as pirate captain carrying her off to his ship made her smile as her heart beat faster. He was smiling back down at her as he stepped through the doorway which led to his bedroom.

'I've been wanting to do this since the morning we met,' he told her, his voice husky with passion and laughter, and Alix realised that their thoughts were again in tune.

'I've been wanting you to do it,' she admitted candidly as he placed her gently on the wide bed. She could be crusadingly independent some other time; right now Jake Hunter was providing the fulfilment of every fantasy she had ever had as he came down beside her, drawing her back into his arms with rough urgency beneath which she could, at last, feel the tenderness which freed her to respond with her whole heart as well as her body.

How they lost their clothes she couldn't remember. She recalled pushing his jacket back from his shoulders and fumbling impatiently with his tie while he muttered something indecipherable as he freed her from her skirt and tights until they were both lying naked together and he was watching her, his hands tangling in the long strands of her hair, which clung with a life of its own to his fingers.

Alix had expected the urgency that was consuming her as well as Jake after so long apart and so much misunderstanding to overwhelm them both. But the wonder of the moment made her pause and she saw that he, too, was caught in it, the miracle that neither of them had been able to believe in.

The face above her twisted almost as if in pain and his hands tightened suddenly on her, holding her against his long, hard body so that she felt her own leap in un-controlled response.

'God, Alix, I love you so much,' he said, and his mouth closed on hers before she could give him any re-sponse except the total surrender she no longer even wanted to withhold.

Afterwards, as they lay quietly together, pulses slowing and heated bodies cooling, he gently brushed back the hair from her damp forehead, a question in his eyes that suddenly didn't need to be spoken aloud.

'Oh, yes, Jake, I love you,' she said softly and realised with amazement when she felt the sudden slackening of tension in the body so close to hers that even now he hadn't been quite sure of her. Somehow this revelation of insecurity in a man who had always seemed to be totally, infuriatingly assured moved her unbearably. She reached up to touch his face and he turned on his back, pulling her to lie with him, her head pillowed against his shoulder.

'I've loved you from that first morning, I think,' she found herself explaining. 'I did try to fight it,' she added more cheerfully, and felt Jake's laughter. Then he stilled, one hand stroking her hair, and she realised he was re-membering what she had said just before the last time they had made love.

'When you said, in that forlorn voice as though some-thing was lost irretrievably, that you had loved me, I couldn't bear it,' he told her, tightening his embrace. 'It sounded so final and so desolate that I had to do some-thing desperate to convince you—and me—that it wasn't

true. I couldn't bear to let you go—and then I had to.'
Remembered pain still touched his voice.

'It's all right,' Alix said urgently, needing to reassure
him and understanding her own feelings clearly for the
first time. 'I was wrong—what's between us is much
stronger than that shell. We can survive more storms
than the world, or the weather, can ever throw at us.'
She reached up to press kisses of comfort to the side of
his neck, his face, and then his mouth, until comfort
flared again into something else entirely and there was
no time for thought, let alone words.

Much later they found time to talk again. Alix was
amazed to remember that they had ever had any diffi-
culty in communicating.

'We'll be married soon,' Jake told her.

She smiled at the familiar autocratic tone. But there
didn't seem much point in arguing with something she
wanted so badly herself. 'Yes,' she agreed, then grinned.
'I'll have to see if Bill will give me away.'

'If he won't, I'll take you anyway,' he warned, not
wholly joking. Then, more seriously, added, 'What about
your work? I'd planned to be based here for a couple
of years——'

'Yes, you were going to tell me your plans, weren't
you?' she remembered, laughing.

'I'm telling you now,' he pointed out. 'Besides, I
wasn't certain what they'd have been if you'd turned me
down,' he added wryly.

'Run away to sea?' she suggested. It was easy to tease,
she discovered, when you felt so secure.

'Something like that—but I'd probably have ab-
ducted you in the process,' he decided, and Alix wasn't
sure that she wouldn't have enjoyed it. Then he came
back to the subject of her work, and if she needed confirmation that she was right to trust Jake it came with
the knowledge that he considered her work as important

as his. 'We could probably still base ourselves mainly in London even when I have to go back to the States to keep an eye on things,' he suggested.

'Or I could get work out there,' she offered, and saw the sudden pleasure in his face and realised he was taking nothing for granted.

'You'd do that?'

'Why not? Or Bill might find himself with an American business section to the paper?' It didn't seem like a big problem to her, not after all they'd come through. 'Or,' hesitantly she voiced the other alternative which had been growing in her mind since his earlier misunderstanding, 'we might start a family?'

His response, a wordless mixture of disbelief swiftly followed by delight and hope, ended in an embrace which lifted her clear of the ground and left her in no doubt of his views on parenthood.

'Children and journalism aren't mutually exclusive,' he pointed out, but Alix didn't need the reassurance that he would not try to confine her ambitions, because she was no longer trapped by her emotions.

'We'll work it out,' she accepted, letting him just hold her. This moment of tranquillity couldn't last, of course. Living with Jake Hunter and not letting him ride rough-shod over her was going to be the biggest challenge she had accepted yet. The thought of the coming years of conflict and passion and laughter was exhilarating, and she laughed aloud, feeling more full of energy than she had in weeks.

Jake looked down at her, understanding glinting in his eyes. 'We'll honeymoon on *Shearwater*,' he decided.

'Oh, yes? Any particular reason?' Not that she needed any for a decision that perfectly fitted in with her own wishes.

He pretended to consider the matter. 'There's an anonymous little island I'd like to revisit.' Shared memories made her smile. 'And you need to practice sail-changing.' Indignation warred with laughter as she turned on him to find both her hands taken in an unbreakable clasp. 'Besides,' he added, drawing her closer, 'you still haven't looked round my cabin, have you?'

'No,' she admitted with assumed indifference, resisting the tug of his hands. 'What's so special about it?'

'The only double bed on the boat,' he chuckled and then, before the thought was even half formed, added, 'and I've never shared it before.'

Somehow it seemed like a wholly unanswerable argument. Not that she wanted to argue. Not at the moment. She let Jake pull her close, surrendering gladly to his demands. She should have known her pirate raider would get what he wanted in the end.

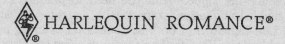

HARLEQUIN®

Don't miss these Harlequin favorites by some of our most
distinguished authors!
And now you can receive a discount by ordering two or more titles!

HT #25525	THE PERFECT HUSBAND by Kristine Rolofson	$2.99	☐
HT #25554	LOVERS' SECRETS by Glenda Sanders	$2.99	☐
HP #11577	THE STONE PRINCESS by Robyn Donald	$2.99	☐
HP #11554	SECRET ADMIRER by Susan Napier	$2.99	☐
HR #03277	THE LADY AND THE TOMCAT by Bethany Campbell	$2.99	☐
HR #03283	FOREIGN AFFAIR by Eva Rutland	$2.99	☐
HS #70529	KEEPING CHRISTMAS by Marisa Carroll	$3.39	☐
HS #70578	THE LAST BUCCANEER by Lynn Erickson	$3.50	☐
HI #22256	THRICE FAMILIAR by Caroline Burnes	$2.99	☐
HI #22238	PRESUMED GUILTY by Tess Gerritsen	$2.99	☐
HAR #16496	OH, YOU BEAUTIFUL DOLL by Judith Arnold	$3.50	☐
HAR #16510	WED AGAIN by Elda Minger	$3.50	☐
HH #28719	RACHEL by Lynda Trent	$3.99	☐
HH #28795	PIECES OF SKY by Marianne Willman	$3.99	☐

Harlequin Promotional Titles

#97122	LINGERING SHADOWS by Penny Jordan	$5.99	☐
	(limited quantities available on certain titles)		

	AMOUNT	$	
DEDUCT:	**10% DISCOUNT FOR 2+ BOOKS**	$	
	POSTAGE & HANDLING	$	
	($1.00 for one book, 50¢ for each additional)		
	APPLICABLE TAXES*	$_____	
	TOTAL PAYABLE	$_____	
	(check or money order—please do not send cash)		

To order, complete this form and send it, along with a check or money order for the
total above, payable to Harlequin Books, to: **In the U.S.:** 3010 Walden Avenue,
P.O. Box 9047, Buffalo, NY 14269-9047; **In Canada:** P.O. Box 613, Fort Erie, Ontario,
L2A 5X3.

Name: _____

Address:_____City: _____

State/Prov.: _____ Zip/Postal Code: _____

*New York residents remit applicable sales taxes.
 Canadian residents remit applicable GST and provincial taxes..

HBACK-JS

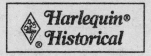

Harlequin® Historical

LOOK TO THE PAST FOR FUTURE FUN AND EXCITEMENT!

The past the Harlequin Historical way, that is. 1994 is going to be a banner year for us, so here's a preview of what to expect:

* The continuation of our bigger book program, with titles such as *Across Time* by Nina Beaumont, *Defy the Eagle* by Lynn Bartlett and *Unicorn Bride* by Claire Delacroix.

* A 1994 March Madness promotion featuring four titles by promising new authors Gayle Wilson, Cheryl St. John, Madris Dupree and Emily French.

* Brand-new in-line series: DESTINY'S WOMEN by Merline Lovelace and HIGHLANDER by Ruth Langan; and new chapters in old favorites, such as the SPARHAWK saga by Miranda Jarrett and the WARRIOR series by Margaret Moore.

* *Promised Brides*, an exciting brand-new anthology with stories by Mary Jo Putney, Kristin James and Julie Tetel.

* Our perennial favorite, the Christmas anthology, this year featuring Patricia Gardner Evans, Kathleen Eagle, Elaine Barbieri and Margaret Moore.

Watch for these programs and titles wherever Harlequin Historicals are sold.

HARLEQUIN HISTORICALS... A TOUCH OF MAGIC!

INDULGE A LITTLE 6947 SWEEPSTAKES
NO PURCHASE NECESSARY

HERE'S HOW THE SWEEPSTAKES WORKS:
The Harlequin Reader Service shipments for January, February and March 1994 will contain, respectively, coupons for entry into three prize drawings: a trip for two to San Francisco, an Alaskan cruise for two and a trip for two to Hawaii. To be eligible for any drawing using an Entry Coupon, simply complete and mail according to directions.

There is no obligation to continue as a Reader Service subscriber to enter and be eligible for any prize drawing. You may also enter any drawing by hand printing your name and address on a 3" x 5" card and the destination of the prize you wish that entry to be considered for (i.e., San Francisco trip, Alaskan cruise or Hawaiian trip). Send your 3" x 5" entries to: Indulge a Little 6947 Sweepstakes, c/o Prize Destination you wish that entry to be considered for, P.O. Box 1315, Buffalo, NY 14269-1315, U.S.A. or Indulge a Little 6947 Sweepstakes, P.O. Box 610, Fort Erie, Ontario L2A 5X3, Canada.

To be eligible for the San Francisco trip, entries must be received by 4/30/94; for the Alaskan cruise, 5/31/94; and the Hawaiian trip, 6/30/94. No responsibility is assumed for lost, late or misdirected mail. Sweepstakes open to residents of the U.S. (except Puerto Rico) and Canada, 18 years of age or older. All applicable laws and regulations apply. Sweepstakes void wherever prohibited.

For a copy of the Official Rules, send a self-addressed, stamped envelope (WA residents need not affix return postage) to: Indulge a Little 6947 Rules, P.O. Box 4631, Blair, NE 68009, U.S.A.

INDR93

- -

INDULGE A LITTLE 6947 SWEEPSTAKES
NO PURCHASE NECESSARY

HERE'S HOW THE SWEEPSTAKES WORKS:
The Harlequin Reader Service shipments for January, February and March 1994 will contain, respectively, coupons for entry into three prize drawings: a trip for two to San Francisco, an Alaskan cruise for two and a trip for two to Hawaii. To be eligible for any drawing using an Entry Coupon, simply complete and mail according to directions.

There is no obligation to continue as a Reader Service subscriber to enter and be eligible for any prize drawing. You may also enter any drawing by hand printing your name and address on a 3" x 5" card and the destination of the prize you wish that entry to be considered for (i.e., San Francisco trip, Alaskan cruise or Hawaiian trip). Send your 3" x 5" entries to: Indulge a Little 6947 Sweepstakes, c/o Prize Destination you wish that entry to be considered for, P.O. Box 1315, Buffalo, NY 14269-1315, U.S.A. or Indulge a Little 6947 Sweepstakes, P.O. Box 610, Fort Erie, Ontario L2A 5X3, Canada.

To be eligible for the San Francisco trip, entries must be received by 4/30/94; for the Alaskan cruise, 5/31/94; and the Hawaiian trip, 6/30/94. No responsibility is assumed for lost, late or misdirected mail. Sweepstakes open to residents of the U.S. (except Puerto Rico) and Canada, 18 years of age or older. All applicable laws and regulations apply. Sweepstakes void wherever prohibited.

For a copy of the Official Rules, send a self-addressed, stamped envelope (WA residents need not affix return postage) to: Indulge a Little 6947 Rules, P.O. Box 4631, Blair, NE 68009, U.S.A.

INDR93

INDULGE A LITTLE
SWEEPSTAKES
OFFICIAL ENTRY COUPON

This entry must be received by: JUNE 30, 1994
This month's winner will be notified by: JULY 15, 1994
Trip must be taken between: AUGUST 31, 1994-AUGUST 31, 1995

YES, I want to win the 3-Island Hawaiian vacation for two. I understand that the prize includes round-trip airfare, first-class hotels and pocket money as revealed on the "wallet" scratch-off card.

Name_____

Address _____ Apt. _____

City_____

State/Prov._____ Zip/Postal Code_____

Daytime phone number_____
             (Area Code)

Account #_____

Return entries with invoice in envelope provided. Each book in this shipment has two entry coupons—and the more coupons you enter, the better your chances of winning!
© 1993 HARLEQUIN ENTERPRISES LTD.   MONTH3